Death and Fondue

Sugar Creek Mystery Series

Book Three

Nova Walsh

Copyright © 2024 by Nova Walsh

All rights reserved.

Published by Two Worlds Press, LLC

Cover art by DLR Cover Designs

www.dlrcoverdesigns.com

No part of this book may be reproduced, or stored in a retrieval system, or transmitted in any form or by any means, electronic, mechanical, photocopying, recording, or otherwise, without express written permission of the publisher.

Published in the United States of America.

First Edition, 2024

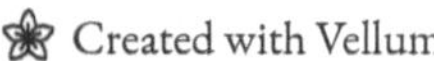 Created with Vellum

Chapter One

Texas is a state of mind.

Truer words were never spoken, if you ask me. Leave it to John Steinbeck to say things eloquently. His quote bounced around my head as I watched the latest gaggle of visitors descend on my Aunt Meg's B&B, Primrose House, midmorning on the first Thursday of August. The group of them bustled in through the front door with roller bags and clicking heels and a seriousness I hadn't experienced since I'd left L.A. back in June.

I'd been at the B&B since early morning, knocking out a load of prep work for a golden anniversary party I was catering the following day which is why I was able to observe the group of tech entrepreneurs firsthand as they landed in Aunt Meg's quaint and cozy farmhouse. The dissonance between Texas cordial and California cool was jarring, to say the least.

"Hey, Barry, check this out," one man said as the group set their laptop bags and purses down on the furniture in the lobby area. He wore a black turtleneck and jeans despite the summer heat. I doubted the getup would last him very long. He'd be in a t-shirt by Saturday. He pointed to a landscape painting of rolling hills of bluebonnets and cattle grazing that hung above the fireplace and guffawed.

"Talk about Podunk. Is this place for real?"

I rolled my eyes as I continued to watch them. The watercolor was one of a limited set from a talented local artist who'd recently had his own retrospective collection in the Modern Art Museum in Fort Worth.

The other man, who must have been Barry, raised an eyebrow and then turned back to his phone without acknowledging the comment. He had thick gray hair and wore designer jeans and an untucked button-down shirt. As well as the most ugly lime green high-tops I'd ever seen, the kind that looked straight out of an 80s movie.

I set out a tray of monster cookies I'd baked that morning, peanut butter and oatmeal mounds bursting with decadent chocolate chunks and dried cherries, and adjusted the tray so it caught the light in an enticing way. Looking up, one woman—the one with platinum blonde hair cut in a fierce bob and wearing a serious navy suit—glanced at the cookies with a scowl.

"Those must be a thousand calories apiece," she mumbled without looking at me, and then she too turned back to her phone.

I reserved my second eye roll and my snarky comments for when I was back in the kitchen by myself. The guest is always right, after all.

The man who'd commented on the painting plopped down onto the lovely blue sofa that sat in the front window next to another much younger man who had thick brown shaggy hair and they both pulled laptops out of their bags. "Hey, what's the Wi-Fi password?" the younger one shouted out to the room. I grabbed one of the printed welcome sheets Aunt Meg had on the check-in desk in the corner and handed it to him. He took it wordlessly without looking at me.

The second woman of the group approached the check-in desk as she pulled a sheaf of papers out of her own laptop bag. She looked to be younger than the rest of them, had long dark brown hair, and was dressed in slim designer jeans and bright red heels so high I couldn't imagine how she got around all day. Those things would have killed my back.

"Are you Margaret? I'm Cheryl, from NexTech Dynamics. I emailed you about our reservation?" Her voice was brisk, but there was an underlying note of fatigue. "I have our itinerary here, and a list of dietary preferences and... um, special requests from the group."

Aunt Meg raised her eyebrows and took the papers the woman handed her without looking at them. "Hi Cheryl. I'm *Meg*. I own Primrose House. We have everything prepared for your stay. Don't you worry about a thing."

The woman gazed around nervously and bit her lip. "It's very important that these requests are met in a timely manner. We are in the middle of a very important decision-making process for our company right now and our people need everything to be exactly right so they can focus on the job at hand. If you cannot accommodate these requests, we'll have to find a place elsewhere..."

Aunt Meg cut her off with a friendly smile. "No, of course. I understand and I'll make sure every item is taken care of if it's in our power to do so. It looks like you've booked five rooms with us for the week. And I see you reserved a suite for a Barry Golding?" Aunt Meg looked over her glasses to the room and the man in the ugly high-tops stuck his hand up without looking up from his phone.

Aunt Meg looked from him to Cheryl, trying to decide who she should be addressing.

"I'll be taking care of everything for the group, so if you could just give me the keys and let me know where to find the rooms, I'll figure it out. Thanks."

Aunt Meg's part-time helper, Maria, came in just then and Aunt Meg motioned her over. "This is Maria," she told the woman. "She's wonderful, and will help you with anything you need during your stay. Maria, do you mind showing our guests to their rooms?"

Maria smiled her warm smile and took the ring of room keys. "If you'll all follow me," she said and waited for the group to collect their things and follow her up the stairs.

"Yo, Eric, your room's ready, man," the turtlenecked one said to the guy still hacking away on his laptop on the couch. He let out a sharp whistle, and I flinched.

The man on the couch, Eric, stood up, his laptop still open and balanced in one hand as he grabbed his stuff and followed the group up the stairs, still staring at the laptop. I hoped he wouldn't fall. The last thing we needed was for one of them to die.

"Woo! You've got your work cut out for you," I told Aunt Meg as I paced the front room.

She frowned as she looked over the sheaf of papers Cheryl had given her. I moved to her side to peer over her shoulder at the strange requests the group had made.

- NO PEANUTS, SEVERE ALLERGY

- on-call theta energy healer

- spirulina and acai for morning smoothies

- bulletproof coffee

- eco friendly organic cleaning products used for all the rooms

- conference space with dedicated Wi-Fi

"Bless their hearts," Aunt Meg said, and we both burst out laughing.

Not that we didn't take their requests seriously, or that we didn't respect every guest that came to stay at Primrose House. We were grateful for their business and would absolutely try to make them comfortable and treat them with hospitality and kindness, like every guest who came through the front door of the B&B. But there are just some things that are not immediately available in a small town in Texas. Like an energy healer, for instance. At least not that I knew of, although times had changed in our little corner of the world, just like everywhere else.

"Good thing they acted like the monster cookies were poison... because to at least one of them they would be," I said. Monster cookies were chock full of peanut butter. I swiftly removed the tray of them from the sideboard. I'd take them home to Cassie, or drop them by the station on my way home. It would give me an excuse to see Ryan Iverson, the sheriff who I was sort of seeing at present, although we hadn't really defined our relationship yet.

"The conference room, at least, won't be a problem," Aunt Meg said. She'd turned the old formal dining room into a meeting area just recently as she'd begun getting more business groups staying at the B&B thanks to a campaign we were running with the Sugar Creek chamber of commerce. It was only one of several new marketing efforts to pump some energy into Aunt Meg's struggling business. Another of them was adding dinner parties and other events, catered by my brand new company, Deep in the Heart Catering.

She nodded. "I guess I could ask around about the healer thing. Georgie might know," Aunt Meg said as she frowned and pulled up the internet. "Or maybe I'll just Google it."

I patted her on the back, not at all envious of the tasks she was about to take on. "I'll get some new cleaning supplies when I stop by the store this afternoon and I'll see what I can do about the food. There are a few more things I have to get for this anniversary party, anyway. If I can't find anything, I guess we could order it to be delivered. Might not get here right away, but we'll do our best, right? And if they have a problem with that, then we will wish them luck and send them on their way. It's okay, Aunt Meg. They probably won't even notice whether half of that stuff is here."

She looked worried despite my reassurance, but nodded as she dived into her search for alternative healers in the hill country. I knew she took her job very seriously and wouldn't rest until every guest was satisfied, no matter how crazy their demands were. Her drive to please every guest was why her B&B had such a great reputation.

Heading back to the kitchen, I thought about what else I needed to get done for the anniversary party I was catering before the end of the day. I'd made three layers of decadent round fudge cakes earlier and they were cooling on wire racks on the sideboard. I would mix up the cherry filling and chocolate icing a little later. Tomorrow, I would fill and ice the cake right before the party.

The menu for the event was simple, but satisfying. Pulled pork with brown sugar caramelized onions, freshly made sweet rolls and cucumber pickles, German potato salad with thin-sliced red onion and capers in a tangy vinaigrette, a Brussels sprout slaw, and garlic green beans for the main event, plus plenty of snacks and tidbits to keep the guests grazing for as long as the party went on. I took a few moments to gather lemon, dill, chives, vinegar, and oil for the dressing I would use for the potato salad, and then chopped through the fragrant herbs.

I'd met the Lancaster family two weeks before, when Maddie Lancaster had called to set the party up for her parents. I was overjoyed to help with the fifty-year anniversary party for fifty people that would take place in the Lancaster backyard—the same place they'd been married so many years before. It was still the height of summer, so it would likely be a warm night. We'd decided on a buffet set up inside the house for guests to come and go as they wished. I wouldn't be servicing this time around, but doing setup and takedown only. I was sad I wouldn't get to see the party in full swing because I always loved to see people enjoying my food, but a job was a job and I was happy for the work.

Since I'd moved back in June, Deep in the Heart Catering had been slowly but steadily growing. A few people in town were still under the mistaken impression that I'd poisoned someone because of an unfortunate funeral I'd catered when I'd first returned to town, but most of the locals had come around quickly and a few nicely worded reviews had helped to get things rolling. I wasn't as busy as I wanted to be, but I was busy enough to keep my little business going, at least for the time being. It would take time, but if I stuck with it, this catering business of mine would grow and eventually thrive. I was certain of it.

Maria came in as I was mixing up the lemon dill vinaigrette for the potato salad.

"Did you get the group squared away?" I asked her as I poured oil in a steady stream with one hand and whisked furiously with the other.

A small smile played on her lips. "Hopefully. They are certainly a needy bunch. They asked for pure ionized mineral water. Do you know if that's what this is?" she asked as she held one of the little plastic bottles we stored in a drink fridge for guests up in the air.

I frowned. "Probably not."

Maria frowned back and folded her arms. "I guess I should go to the store."

I finished with the vinaigrette and used a funnel to pour it into a dressing container so I could easily use it the next day. "No, it's okay. I'm heading over there now, anyway, and I can get water and the other stuff on their list. I'll try, at least."

Maria smiled. "Thank you, I appreciate it. I don't know why it matters, exactly what kind of water we have. You would think that bottled water would be good enough. Even tap water here is good enough for me."

I raised my eyebrows and cleaned up the kitchen quickly, then hung my apron on a hook in the pantry. "I don't know. They might be testing us. Or maybe they really believe there's something bad in the other water. Who knows? Doesn't matter. Like Aunt Meg says, the guest comes first. I shouldn't take too long, I only have a few things to buy for the party tomorrow. Call me if they ask for anything else while I'm gone."

As I grabbed my keys and purse and headed out the kitchen door with my trusty notebook, I was assaulted with a wave of air so hot it felt like I'd stepped into an oven. Good old Texas summer, there was nothing quite like it. Too bad there was so much of it.

August was always the worst. It was right in the middle of the heat. You'd already gotten your fill and yet you knew there were still a couple more months to endure before it would even hint at cooling off. I pushed my sweaty hair off my face as I headed toward my car in the gravel parking lot in the front of the B&B.

It would be a long few days with the California people. I could feel the storm coming. At least *I* didn't have to cater to their every whim. My only official catering job for them would be a group dinner they had planned at Wild Hare Winery for Saturday night. I sat a moment as the air conditioning in my car struggled to life and made a couple of notes to myself about meeting with Cheryl later to hammer out the details for the event. I'd only gotten a brief idea of what they'd had in mind for their dinner when they'd booked the reservation, and I needed to cement it all down with her when I returned from the store.

But one problem at a time, I told myself as I backed out of the parking lot and turned toward downtown Sugar Creek.

One problem at a time.

Chapter Two

Later that evening, I pulled in back of my best friend Cassie's shop, Divine Finds, and around to her little cottage where I was currently living. Cassie was an amazing friend, always willing to help me out. As soon as I'd told her I was moving back to Sugar Creek from the bustle of Los Angeles earlier in the summer, she'd demanded that I move in with her until I got on my feet. Two months later, I was still living with her and had made no real plans to change that.

My phone dinged as I cut the engine, and I looked down to see a text from Ryan Iverson.

Hey, honey. Sorry, I can't get off work tonight after all. Want to come over on Sunday? Or we could go to a movie?

My heart sank for just a moment, but I shrugged it off. When I'd stopped by the station on my way home, Ryan had been out on a call, so I hadn't gotten the chance to see him, although everyone at the station had loved my cookies.

The sheriff and I had been dating ever since I'd come back to Texas. It hadn't taken long for the two of us to become nearly joined at the hip, at least when one or the other of us wasn't working. Unfortunately, because of the nature of his work and mine, we didn't see nearly as much of each other as I would have liked and things were still very up in the air between us as far as what our relationship actually was.

I texted back. *Sunday is good, but maybe on the later side? Not sure how long my event's going to go on Saturday. I'll let you know.* I signed off with a kiss emoji, even though it still made me a little uncomfortable. It had only been a couple of months since the man nearly arrested me, but we'd made our peace around my poor snooping choices and he and I were definitely hitting it off in the romance department.

I stretched as I stood from the car and tucked my phone into my purse. I was weary from the day's kitchen work, but excited to get yet another event under my belt. Grabbing a bowl with extra potato salad and a hunk of sharp cheddar I'd picked up at the store, I closed the door with my hip. I figured gourmet grilled cheese sandwiches and potato salad would be a perfect dinner for Cassie and me. With any luck we'd be able to watch the next episode of Only Murders in the Building, which we'd been binge-watching every chance we got.

I'd tried to sit down with Cheryl at the B&B after I returned from my shopping trip earlier, but was informed that the Next-Tech group was in meetings for the rest of the afternoon and not to be bothered, so I'd have to wait to nail down the details of their dinner the following day. I'd found the special mineral water they'd requested as well as the ingredients for their bulletproof coffee, including grass fed butter and MCT oil, and new cleaning supplies at the local H.E.B., but no spirulina or acai. Those would have to come from the internet.

Our dog Cocoa immediately bounced around me as I pushed the cottage door open. He had a sixth sense for anyone arriving, and he must have been waiting for me by the door. I laughed as I tried to navigate through the room without stepping on the little guy.

"Cocoa, honey. You're gonna take me out!"

Cassie whistled to him from the kitchen. "Cocoa, come get a treat!"

He immediately abandoned me and my armful of food and trotted over to Cassie to claim his reward. I put the food down on the kitchen counter and went over to give him a proper belly rub. It was a good feeling, having a creature so happy to see me. I rewarded him for his enthusiasm with another dog treat and then straightened, stretching out my sore back some more.

Cocoa had inserted himself into our lives at a festival I'd worked a few weeks before. After we tried our best to find his owner with no luck, Cassie and I had made him part of our crew. Good thing, because he'd helped to save us from calamity after we'd gotten ourselves into deep trouble while looking into the murder of a city councilman. Cocoa was as scruffy as ever, a delightful little mutt with an adorable charm. He had the look of a dog who's lived a tale or two. His fur, a delightful mix of tawny brown and soft wheat, was perpetually tousled and unkempt. We had no clue what breed he was, but there was a hint of terrier in the way his ears perked up—one cocked slightly higher than the other—as if always tuned into the secrets of Sugar Creek.

"Ugh. I'm exhausted." I kicked my kitchen clogs off and settled down on the barstool to watch Cassie. "How was your day?"

She smiled as she threw some lemon slices into a pitcher of freshly made tea. "Pretty good. I'm happy tomorrow's Friday. Can't wait to go hit up some sales."

Cassie was a modern day treasure hunter, and weekends were her real jam. She visited estate sales, antique bizarres, junkyards, and everything in between to supply her own store with amazing vintage finds. I'd been too busy to go with her lately, but I'd dipped my toe into the estate sale madness when she'd taken me a couple of months back to look for kitchen supplies for my business, and I was hooked too.

"Wish I could go with! I've got my work cut out for me though with the rest of the anniversary party and this dinner for

Aunt Meg's latest arrivals on Saturday. I don't even know what I'm going to do for that yet. Nobody was available to talk about it today. Boy, Cass, you should have seen this group!" I told her as I stood and grabbed the potato salad and cheese and headed into the kitchen to make us some grub. "Aunt Meg's going to have her hands full, that's for sure. They asked for an on-call energy healer," I said with a giggle.

"What's that?" she asked.

"I have no idea. Their admin came in with a list of demands, like she was a hostage negotiator. Actually, she seemed nice enough. But the rest of the group..." I waved my hands in the air, completely at a loss for words to describe them.

Cassie laughed. "You know even the hardest people fall to Aunt Meg's charms. She'll be fine, I'm sure. Especially when Bertie gets here. Those two are a force to be reckoned with!"

I let out a little squeal at the thought. I'd called Aunt Meg's favorite cousin, Cousin Roberta, or Bertie as we all knew her, a few weeks back and made plans to have her drive over from the Houston area to surprise Aunt Meg for her birthday. She was supposed to arrive sometime the following morning. We'd even booked her a room at the B&B under the name Lyle Lovett, which had given the three of us a good laugh when we'd decided on it over the phone. But that was before I realized I'd be subjecting Bertie to a group of fussy tech people. I felt bad because I knew that Aunt Meg would be focused on making them all happy and wouldn't be able to relax with Bertie. Knowing Bertie, though, *she* would find it all fascinating. She loved to meet new people. I just hoped she and Bertie would have enough time to catch up properly with everything going on.

Pulling out a loaf of leftover sourdough, I cut four thick slices and buttered them on one side. Next, I sliced thin pieces of red onion and tomato and heated a skillet. Cassie sat at the barstool and rubbed her foot along Cocoa's belly. He had a knack for knowing just where to lie to get attention.

"Are you going to be out all night tomorrow night? What time does your gig end?" Cassie asked as she watched me cook.

"It's a drop off thing, so I need to set up at five and then take down at nine, but I was thinking about stopping by the B&B in between to help Aunt Meg out a little and visit with Bertie. You wanna come over too?"

Cassie's cheeks flushed. "I was thinking about asking Ty if he wanted to come over and watch a movie, actually. Maybe get some takeout. We haven't seen each other much lately."

My heart sank, and I immediately felt guilty. Her boyfriend, deputy Ty Clayburn, was one of the sweetest men I knew. I was so happy Cassie had snagged him. But I also had a feeling that having me living with her was getting in the way of their alone time and I hated that I was keeping them apart. "I'm so sorry, Cass. Of course I'll be gone. I can stay over there for the night if you want. You tell me any time you two want to be alone. I don't mind at all."

"It's fine, really. You don't need to stay the night over there. I just wanted to know what your plans were."

I wondered yet again if it might not be time to get a place of my own. Every time I'd mentioned it, Cassie had put up a fight, but I hadn't really thought how having a roommate must be putting a damper on Cassie's budding relationship. The two of them were always so nice about everything, so considerate, and I realized that even if I *was* getting in their way, they would never come right out and say it. That was not good at all. I silently vowed to start looking for a place just as soon as the next round of event chaos had passed. The last thing on earth I wanted was to be a nuisance for my friend, who had already done so much for me.

The skillet was warm, so I quickly sautéed the onions in a bit of butter and then slid the bread onto the pan. Cutting thick slices of cheddar, I placed them onto the bread and then layered on the onions and tomatoes and closed the sandwiches up to let them toast.

"I can see your brain smoking," Cassie said as she fiddled with a pair of nail clippers. "You better not be thinking about moving out, lady."

I shrugged and spun the spatula around and around in my hand, not meeting her gaze. "It's not right. I've been here too long. We're grown women, and you need your own space."

She reached over and grabbed my free hand, and I raised my eyes to hers. "I like you here, Abby. I really do. And not just because you make the best food in town. I enjoy having your friendship to come home to. It's so much nicer to walk into this place every night and know that I'll have someone to talk to, someone to laugh with. Before you came back, I was pretty lonely."

"You had Ty," I told her.

She shook her head. "Ty is fantastic. I love him, I truly do. But he is not here every night. And he's not as good at gabbing, anyhow. Don't you dare move out on me, you hear? I need you. Sure, I need some alone time now and then. But that's fine. We can work it out, like we're doing right now."

I gave her a small smile as I flipped the sandwiches and scooped potato salad onto two plates.

"Okay, but only if you're really sure. I don't want to get in the way of anything with you two."

Cassie laughed. "We're fine, trust me. We can hang out at his place any time we want. But it's nice to have him over here sometimes. Just the two of us."

It was my turn to blush. "You promise to tell me anytime, okay? I will book myself a hotel room or stay with Aunt Meg or whatever I need to do."

"That isn't necessary. Just a few hours tomorrow night is all I'm asking."

I scooped the grilled cheeses onto the cutting board and cut them into triangles with a loud crunch. Delicious melted cheese oozed out of the sides and I scooped each one up with the spatula and put them on the plates, then handed one to Cassie.

"Okay, will do. It'll be at least ten by the time I get done with the anniversary party cleanup."

I felt a little better about staying after Cassie's reassurance, but not completely. I knew that eventually I would need to find my own place. But for tonight, I would lean into the roommate vibes. As Cassie plopped down on the couch and grabbed the remote, Cocoa pushed himself between the couch and the coffee table and spread out beneath our legs. He knew better than to get up on the couch with us when we were eating, but he also knew enough to be right in place for any crumbs or last bites that might fall in his direction.

"Really, Abby," Cassie said as she leaned over and rested her head on my shoulder for a minute, her curly blonde hair surrounding me and making me giggle. "I love having you here. It's been super fun."

I snuggled into her. "Same here. I love you, Cass."

CHAPTER THREE

The next morning I ran over to Fredericksburg before I headed to Primrose House, hoping that the bigger town might carry the spirulina and acai. I'd gotten so wrapped up in watching our show the night before, I'd forgotten to place an order for the exotic supplies online and I was worried it was too late. I guessed that by now the California group would be up and needy, so I hustled, wanting to head off any complaints if I could. The less trouble Aunt Meg had to deal with, the better. Luckily, Fredericksburg had a health food store, and I was in and out with the ingredients and headed back to Sugar Creek within a few minutes.

Hopefully, this would be the last of the strange requests. Between the anniversary party I would cater in a few hours, the big unknown of the dinner party for the California group the following night, and Bertie coming into town for Aunt Meg's birthday, I was up to my eyeballs in work and planning. The less I got added to my plate, the better.

I was happy to see the parking lot of the B&B fairly empty still when I pulled in a little while later. The drive from Houston would take Bertie hours, but I also knew she was a very early riser. I hadn't heard from her yet, so I doubted she was in Sugar Creek already, but I would kick myself if I didn't get to witness the reunion first hand.

"Morning!" I called as I came in through the front door. The lobby was empty except for Maria, who was dusting the bookshelves.

"Oh, good. I was hoping I could talk to you a minute." Holding out the bag, I smiled. "I got the rest of the stuff for the group."

"That's wonderful, thank you. The blonde woman was down earlier asking for a smoothie. I will tell her we have it now."

I grabbed her arm before she left. "One other thing," I said, lowering my voice.

She raised an eyebrow and leaned in.

"Cassie and I have a surprise for Aunt Meg coming today. Her cousin Bertie is going to stay through Aunt Meg's birthday. We booked her a room under a false name. She should be here soon. I was hoping you and I could work together to keep Aunt Meg's load as light as possible the next few days, so she has time to be with Bertie."

Maria gave me a wide smile. "That is lovely. I would be honored to help."

I nodded. "Okay, if you need help or have any problems, come to me if I'm here or call me if I'm not. Let's give her as much of a birthday vacation as possible."

Maria headed off to make smoothies, and I glanced out at the parking lot. Still no sign of Bertie, so I made my way back to the dining room turned conference room to see if I could find Cheryl. I was getting really worried about not having a plan for the dinner party the following night.

The door was open, so I stuck my head in. The room was fairly small, but the oval dining table for eight seemed to work well enough for most of the business groups that had stayed with us so far. All three of the men from the California group huddled at the opposite end of the table from the door, glaring at each other.

"This is a terrible idea, Barry. You know we'll get ten times more money if we take the company public rather than selling to this tiny no-name group. I don't understand you! Why are you being so pigheaded about this?" the older one said, his voice low and angry. His face was blazing red, but it could have been because he was still wearing a turtleneck. It was fifty-fifty whether he was hopping mad or simply overheated.

"Kevin, I've had just about enough out of you! Why don't you go start your own company if you're so sure you know how to run things? It's going to be this way, whether you like it or not. End of discussion."

The third man, the younger one, Eric, glanced from one to the other nervously. "Hey, why don't we just back up? Take a breath..." The two older men glared at him and he turned quickly back to his laptop.

I made a movement by the door, not wanting to startle them, and all three looked in my direction. I flushed scarlet, feeling guilty for interrupting.

"Sorry, I was just looking for Cheryl?"

"I think she's in her room," Eric said with a smile. I was shocked that he'd actually made eye contact. It was the first time in twenty-four hours I hadn't seen his face buried in a screen.

"Thanks," I said and backed away quietly. The other two ignored me and went back to their conversation. I heard their raised voices as I headed back to the front of the house. I hoped they wouldn't break anything. The tension that wafted off these people was intense, and I could see why they needed their energy healed. I couldn't imagine having to work with such stress all the time. No, thank you.

Before I could move toward the stairs to the rooms, I saw Cheryl pacing in the yard in front of the house. I smiled as I made my way outside, and squinted in the late morning sun, reveling for a moment in that delicious difference between the air conditioning and the heat of a summer day. Alas, the feeling didn't last long, and soon I was hotter than a billy goat in a pepper patch.

"Hi, Cheryl?" I said as I headed the woman's direction.

She startled as I approached and I felt bad for a moment that I'd interrupted whatever she'd been doing. She looked lost in thought. Or maybe simply lost.

I wondered how she'd gotten wrapped up with the rest of this group. She seemed distracted, and a little entitled, sure, but unlike the rest of them, she wasn't totally absorbed in screens and arguments. She was young, though. Young enough to not be totally jaded. Maybe that was the difference. She wrapped her arms around herself as if she were cold despite the scorcher of a day.

"Hi, I'm Abby. I do the catering for Primrose House. I was hoping we could talk about the dinner party for tomorrow night. But if you're busy right now..." I trailed off, not wanting to give her an excuse but also not wanting to cause the young woman any more distress.

"Oh, right." She shook her head like she was trying to clear cobwebs and gave me a smile. "Yeah, the dinner party."

"I know you said you wanted a plated dinner, but I was wondering if you'd be open to something a little different." The idea of fondue had been playing in my mind ever since I'd put the dinner party on the books and I couldn't shake it. Summer wasn't exactly the best time for bubbling pots of molten cheese, but I thought it would be a change of pace for the group, something a little more festive than a plated dinner would be. They probably had plated dinners all the time. I knew this kind of crowd valued their team building. What could build a team faster than sharing a delicious pot of cheese?

Cheryl frowned. "I don't know," she said nervously. "What do you have in mind?"

"I was thinking about doing fondue. We could do a couple of

pots on the table, have a buffet of sorts for dipping, bread, veggies, that sort of thing. Maybe one cheese, one chocolate."

She raised one eyebrow. "This sounds very heavy. We have one vegetarian and one keto in the group. It might be better to..."

"I could do a keto version, and the cheese and chocolate would be vegetarian. I could do a couple of salads too for anybody who wants to keep it lighter..."

Could I do a keto version of fondue? I mentally crossed my fingers that I'd be able to figure it out by tomorrow.

Before she could respond, the crunch of tires on the gravel drive grabbed both of our attention. Cheryl glanced down at her phone and then up at the car that was pulling in. "I'm sorry, but I've got to go. But yeah, okay, fondue. Why not? Just make sure there are plenty of options."

I watched the car pull in, and when I realized it wasn't Bertie, I glanced back at Cheryl, who was heading quickly toward the house. She shot one last look at the parking lot just before walking inside. I turned back and saw a couple were emerging from the car. These two must be the other reservation Primrose House had for the weekend. Between the Californians, the couple who'd just arrived, and the reservation we'd made for Bertie, the house was full up for the weekend, which made me happy. Aunt Meg needed all the business she could get, even if it would create more chaos and work. At least I didn't have any catering jobs on the books other than the anniversary party and the dinner party the following night, so I would be free to help.

I only hoped these two wouldn't be as much of a handful as the other group of B&B guests were proving to be. The steps of the front porch creaked as they made their way inside with their luggage and I bit my lip. Only time would tell.

Chapter Four

I waited a few minutes after the couple went inside before I followed. It was hot, but I needed time to myself to think. I was fretting suddenly. What if pushing the fondue thing was a bad idea? The California group was overly health conscious, that was obvious. And we were smack dab in the middle of Texas summer, not exactly Swiss Alps ski resort kind of weather. But something about the idea of it just really tickled me, and not only because I'd found a vintage set of fondue pots at an estate sale I'd been to with Cassie recently and was itchy to use them. My creative side was hankering to play with the idea of fondue, see what kind of unusual combinations I might come up with. The idea energized me.

But could I force people to take part in my whims just for the sake of my creativity? I frowned and studied the ground as I walked slowly back inside. My business sense said don't do it. But I felt very low interest in listening to my business sense at present.

"Looks like you'll be staying with us until Tuesday?" Aunt Meg asked the couple as I stepped inside. They stood in front of her desk as I walked in and I got a good look at them. He had neatly cut dark brown hair and hers was long sun-kissed waves held out of her face by designer sunglasses pushed up on her head. Their attire was effortlessly smart-casual and screamed money—the kind of money I could only dream of. The man wore a well-fitting polo and khakis, and the woman wore a chic sundress and tasteful sandals. They both seemed quite a bit more relaxed than our other guests, which I took as a good sign.

"That's right, we'll check out Tuesday morning. We have a midday flight back home."

Perfect. Both groups would leave on Tuesday morning. I'd planned a birthday bash for Aunt Meg for Tuesday night, so we were in the clear. I was happy she would have an empty house for the celebration. We could focus all our efforts on her, and she could truly enjoy her party.

"Where's home for y'all?" she asked as she handed the man the key to the downstairs suite.

"California," the woman replied as she dug through her purse for something.

"Oh, we have another group from California with us! What a coincidence!"

Uh oh. The possibility of these two having additional requests or drama for us skyrocketed. I felt like we were up to our eyeballs in problems, as it was. I reminded myself that just because they were from the Golden State, it didn't mean they were as demanding as the others.

"We're from Southern California, San Diego," the man added.

"And what brought you to Sugar Creek, if I might ask?"

"It's our anniversary. And my sister recommended this area to us," the man replied. The couple glanced at each other and the man smiled.

"Well, I hope you enjoy your stay! There's a winery right down the road from us if you want to check it out, Wild Hare Winery. It's a little hot to walk, but I can call you a car if you need it. And there are several delicious restaurants on Main Street. We have a happy hour every afternoon from four to six here in the front room."

"Oh, that's alright," the man replied. "We have a car to get around. And we'll check out the winery. Thank you."

Aunt Meg gestured to them both with a smile. "Follow me, Mr. and Mrs. Hildebrand. I'll show you where the room is."

The three of them headed down the hallway and I turned back to stare out at the parking lot. I bit my lip again, still worrying over the question of fondue but excited for Bertie to arrive too. What was taking her so long?

"You expecting a delivery or something, girl? Is Ryan supposed to come over?" Aunt Meg asked a few minutes later, making me jump. I hadn't realized she'd come back into the room.

I shook my head absentmindedly as I paced in front of the window. I couldn't help myself. I looked out at the parking lot again.

"Well, whatcha doin'? You've been checking the lot every five minutes! What are you up to?"

I turned to her and smiled. "Nothing, nothing. Just thinking. Sorry." I would feel so bad if I gave the surprise away, but I was seriously struggling to keep a hold of my excitement.

The blonde woman from the business group came down the stairs just then, interrupting my thoughts. She strode toward Aunt Meg and my blood pressure tipped upward in anticipation of trouble.

"I'm sorry, but it's really just totally unhealthy to sit down all day. Are you sure there's no way we can get some standing desks in here?" the woman said as she tucked a straight lock of hair behind her ear. I think she tried to smile, as if she was being friendly, but the thing she did with her mouth scared me.

"I wish we could. And it's something we will absolutely look into for the future, but I'm sorry. Right now, this is all we've got," Aunt Meg told her. I was so happy that she was pushing back some. These people could deal with a little adversity. It might do them some good to not get every single thing they wanted. But I knew it was hard for her to say no to any request, no matter how unreasonable. I gave her a warm smile of support and she returned it.

The woman blew out a breath and shrugged her shoulders. "Is there a coffee shop in this godforsaken town?"

"Of course, there's a wonderful place right down on Main Street. Sugar Creek Bakery has the best coffee in this part of Texas," Aunt Meg told her.

The woman rolled her eyes. "Oh, great. A bakery, what a shocker. Can't go anywhere around here without being assaulted by sugar and gluten. I guess there's no hope of a Starbucks."

"Maybe over in Fredericksburg, but that's a bit of a drive," Aunt Meg told her.

She pulled out her phone. "You have Uber here, don't you? Please tell me you people have Uber."

"You going to a coffeeshop, Tori? Can I come with?" Eric said as he came down the hall in a rush, slinging the strap of his computer bag over his head.

Her face turned hard. "No, Eric. I need to work alone. You know that. Find your own coffeeshop." She grabbed her bag and slammed out the front door without giving him another glance.

Eric frowned and watched her go, then removed the laptop bag and harrumphed over to the couch by the window. More than once he looked out the window at the woman on the porch, his face a mixture of pain and something else. I wondered, was he was interested in her romantically? Or was something else brewing there? I couldn't get a good enough read on him to know, but it wasn't nothing.

Before I had much time to think about it, I spied Roberta's SUV pull into the parking lot and I tried my best not to let out a whoop. I really wanted Aunt Meg to be surprised, and giving it away would ruin everything.

I texted Cassie. *The Bertie has landed!*

She sent back celebratory emojis. *Wish I was there. Hug her for me. I'll be done here in a couple of hours. I'll try to come over but have a lot to put away today!*

Aunt Meg was sitting at the desk in the corner, doing paperwork. Her eyeglasses slipped down her nose.

"Looks like you've got another guest," I told her as Bertie pulled a massive suitcase up the steps. I was nearly hopping with excitement.

Aunt Meg looked up from the screen with a frown and sighed. "Do you mind checking them in for me? I'm in the middle of..."

"Oh, you hoo!" Bertie cried as she stepped inside. "It's Lyle Lovett, here for my B&B stay!"

"Bertie!" Aunt Meg cried and jumped up to hug her cousin.

Roberta was a hoot. Just as spunky as Aunt Meg, but with a full head of wildly curly grey hair and a little more sass. I'd always loved her.

"I'm not Bertie," she said with a laugh as she pulled away and moved to me for a hug. "I'm Lyle Lovett!"

"Well, mystery solved!" Aunt Meg said with a laugh. "I had a feeling we weren't actually going to be graced with a star's presence when I took that reservation. There would have been more hoopla. More demands."

"Isn't that the truth?" I said as I squeezed Bertie tight. She'd often visited us when I was a kid, and her presence was always something to look forward to. "I thought it would be a nice surprise to bring her up for the week for your birthday," I told Aunt Meg.

There were tears in Aunt Meg's eyes and a wide smile on her face. "You are too kind, baby girl. It's too much."

"Oh, just you wait! Birthday celebrations are in the works. This is nothing!"

She wiped her eyes and hugged Bertie again. "I'm so glad you're here. Thanks for making the drive."

"Are you kidding? I'm thrilled! But I want the royal treatment, spa day, winery tour. The works! I saw that flashy new website you've got. Made me all sorts of excited for a visit."

Aunt Meg laughed. "We've been working hard to drum up business. And for sure, we can do some of the fun stuff! But I've got a pretty full house right now, unfortunately."

"With a bunch of needy people," I added.

Aunt Meg nodded. "So I won't have too much time to mess around. But you're welcome to get the royal treatment on your own! Or with Abby here!"

I eyed Bertie, trying to send her silent messages. We'd talked some about how I was planning on taking over the B&B tasks more while Bertie was in town, so she knew Aunt Meg would be more free than she realized. I'd also set them up with a spa day in Fredericksburg on Tuesday, figuring that by then most of the B&B work would have tapered off and we would follow with a big birthday bash on Tuesday evening before Bertie had to leave us and another wave of guests descended.

"Oh, well. You'll just have to live vicariously then, I suppose!" Bertie said with a laugh.

Aunt Meg swatted her leg. "You're just as feisty as ever, I see."

Bertie tilted her head back and laughed. "Got me there. I'm like a fine wine, I get more condensed with time. Is that how it goes?"

After a few more minutes, I left them to catch up. I was nearly ready for the anniversary party, but I had to pack everything up and get it over to the Lancaster residence by five. I'd borrowed the Connolys' VW van once again since I had so much to take over, which made me feel mighty guilty, but I still hadn't had time or money to find a vehicle of my own that worked for catering. The couple never seemed to mind though, and I always brought it back with a full tank of gas as a thank you.

As I put the finishing touches on the beautiful cherry chocolate cake for the party, piping swirls of chocolate and layering in the homemade cherry filling, I finally made my decision for the dinner party the following night. Fondue it would be. Not only was I sure I could get all the ingredients I needed on short notice, I liked the challenge of bringing the Californians around to the joys of a good runny cheese and bread.

Besides, it was going to be at a winery. What went better with wine than fondue?

I ran back in to say goodbye to Aunt Meg and Bertie before I headed out to set up the party. They sat together on the blue couch, leaning in close to each other and laughing like they were sharing a few good secrets. I was so happy I'd asked her down for Aunt Meg's birthday.

"You two have fun! I'll be back in an hour or so. Then we can make plans for the big birthday bash!"

"Hold your horses there, girl!" Aunt Meg cried. "I did not agree to any birthday bash!"

Bertie and I laughed at her. "You couldn't stop us if you tried, honey," Bertie said.

"That's right, Aunt Meg. Sometimes you need to just sit back and let yourself be pampered. And your birthday is one of those times."

I headed out the door quickly before she could protest anymore. Not only would it do her no good, I had a party to cater. Time to get the show on the road.

Chapter Five

After setting up the anniversary party for the Lancaster family, I quickly headed over to Cassie's place. I knew she and Ty were planning for alone time, but I wanted to pick up Cocoa and take him over to meet Bertie. I'd texted Cassie before I left the party to make sure it was okay and she'd told me that Ty hadn't come over yet, so I hightailed it to the cottage to pick up our scruffy mutt.

"Hey, Cass!" I called as I headed into the cottage. I smelled homemade marinara and knew Ty was in for a special treat. Cassie's marinara was famous and irresistible when she poured it over manicotti and baked it. My mouth watered, but I ignored it. Maybe if I was lucky, there would be leftovers later.

"Hey, Abby! How's Bertie? Gosh, I wish I could go over and hang out. There was just too much to do after I got back. Couldn't fit it in."

"Don't worry about it! You are gonna have a great night with Ty. Bertie will still be there tomorrow. Wow, it smells amazing in here."

"Thanks, I got a cooking bug," she told me with a laugh.

"Well, I won't keep you. Just thought it would be fun to take Cocoa over to the B&B for a while."

She nodded. "I'm sure he'll love it." She pulled his leash out of the coat closet and handed it to me, even though we rarely used it. Cocoa had no interest in leaving our sides most of the time, but we used the leash to reassure others he was under control.

"Alright, have fun tonight," I said, and gave her a wink. She blushed and swatted at me, and I laughed as we headed out the door.

Cocoa was overjoyed to be going to Primrose House. Over the last couple of months he'd really made himself a part of our group and he very often accompanied me to Primrose House or hung out in the shop with Cassie. He was good at keeping quiet and most of the time people either didn't notice him or fell in love with him right away. I knew Bertie would get a kick out of him. He was high energy and spunky, just like she was.

And as we walked in the door of Primrose House a little while later, I saw my hunch was right. He immediately headed to Bertie on the couch and jumped up next to her, ready to greet the new person in his life. Somehow, he always seemed to know who would be amenable to his kisses and who wouldn't. It was quite the skill.

"Oh, my goodness! Who is this lovely little fellow?" She laughed as Cocoa jumped into her lap and started to lick her all over, tail going a mile a minute.

"Cocoa, good grief!" I told him. "Give Bertie some space. She might run out of air!"

He stepped off of her and sat on the couch, tail still wagging furiously, a gleeful grin on his face. Bertie leaned in and hugged him, then pet his head. He soaked up the limelight like the attention hound that he was.

"This is Cocoa. He attached himself to me at a festival I was catering at a couple months back. We tried to find his owner, but no luck, so now he's part of our crew."

"And we're happy to have him," Aunt Meg said. She stroked Cocoa's back and his tongue lolled. He was one satisfied critter.

I settled into the vintage green wingback chair next to the couch, where Aunt Meg and Bertie sat with Cocoa between them. "Alright, what have I missed?"

Aunt Meg's eyes went wide. "Bertie has some big news. You wanna tell her, Bertie?"

"It's big, but I'm sorry to say it isn't very positive. Rick and I are getting a divorce."

My hand went to my mouth. "Oh, no. Bertie. I'm so sorry. That's terrible."

She shrugged and stroked Cocoa's fur. "It's been hard, that's no lie. But honestly, I'm happy to be rid of him. He's been trying unsuccessfully to cheat on me for years now. The latest one turned out to be some computer scam. He told me he was in love with someone from Uganda. He said she loved him and wanted him to move over there with her. So I told him, 'Uganda be kidding me,' you know... you gotta..." she threw her head back and laughed and Aunt Meg and I laughed too. Cocoa wagged his tail. Like I said, Bertie was a hoot.

"Anyhoo... that was the last straw. I told him if he wanted to be with someone else that he could find her without me cooking his dinner and washing his clothes anymore and I packed my things and went down to our summer house in Spoonbill Bay. Thank goodness we have it still. Good luck to whoever ends up with him, if anyone'll even take him." She shrugged and rolled her eyes.

She seemed to be upbeat about it, but I knew she must be hurting on the inside.

"How are Sarah and Bobby taking it?" I asked. Her grown children had been like cousins to me and my brother growing up. We didn't talk often, but I still thought of them fondly.

"The kids took it pretty hard. At least they're all grown and out on their own. But it's never easy. They've been visiting me on the weekends, one at a time. I think they're worried about me. But honestly, I'm having the time of my life right now!"

"The beach certainly seems to agree with you," Aunt Meg told her with a smile. "You're looking as young and spunky as ever."

Bertie nodded. "I'm getting a lot more exercise, walking the beach, walking to the market. I even tried yoga at the senior center the other day!"

Before we could continue our conversation, Barry and the older man, Kevin, came into the room. "I don't like it, man. I'm telling you, it's a waste! Why don't you want this business to succeed?" Kevin said to Barry. He was right on the other man's heels, close enough to trip him. There was a fiery anger in his eyes, a hatred even.

Barry shrugged him off for a moment, and then wheeled on him with an icy glare. "I do want NexTech to succeed. But I want it my way and if you can't trust me, then it's time for you to leave!"

"I'm not going anywhere, Barry. I own almost as much of NexTech as you do. You don't have as much power as you think you do. I could go to the board..."

Barry turned away from him and as he did, caught a glimpse of Cocoa on the couch with Bertie. "What on earth is that ugly thing?" Heading straight for the happy hour setup, he grabbed a wine glass. He eyed Cocoa with disgust and a rumble began deep in Cocoa's throat.

I shot Cocoa a frown, and he quieted, lying down beside Bertie with his hands on his paws, but his eyes followed the CEO with an intensity that surprised me. Clearly, Cocoa was not a fan of Barry. Or maybe he just really hated Barry's lime green shoes. I knew *I* sure did.

"Since when did this place allow pets?" he said as he grazed through the fruits and cheeses I'd set out and popped a grape into his mouth. "I thought Cheryl made sure to get us an animal-free place."

Kevin frowned at the interruption to their argument, but silently grabbed a plate and piled it with cheese and veggies.

My face turned bright red. "I'm sorry, sir. Cocoa is mine. He's just visiting for a few minutes."

Barry stared at me for a long moment and popped another grape into his mouth. "I'm allergic to animals."

Really? I wanted to ask. *All animals?* Instead I said, "I'll take him outside. I didn't realize. Come on, Cocoa." I patted my leg and the little guy hopped off the couch and dutifully followed me toward the front door. But not without giving Barry one more low growl as he passed the man. I had to try really hard to keep the smile from my face. Good old Cocoa wasn't going to go without at least a little fight.

I got the distinct impression that Barry had simply complained about Cocoa because he was unhappy and wanted everyone else around him to be too. Certainly, everyone who worked for him seemed to be unhappy.

As I stepped out onto the porch with Cocoa, I found the couple sitting together on the porch swing enjoying a glass of wine. A little further down the porch, Cheryl sat in a rocker with a book and a cup of tea. I was happy that at least someone from their group was taking some time away from the stress and intensity of the business affairs to relax. I realized that she probably wasn't as involved in the company as the rest of the group was. A personal assistant or admin who was probably not paid very well, I would guess.

The sun was just setting, but the heat was still making itself known. I wondered what to do with Cocoa. I didn't want to take him back to Cassie's place and interrupt her date night. But I didn't want to leave him outside in the heat either.

"Oh, aren't you a cute thing?" Cheryl said as Cocoa trotted over to her, his tongue hanging out. She pet his head and I was pleased to see a genuine smile on her face. He was happy to lean into the attention once again.

"Watch out, he might lick you to death," I told her with a laugh as I propped myself against the porch rail and gazed out at the yard bathed in a purple and pink light from the mottled sky. We often got big rainstorms in the summer, but it had been parched lately. I prayed that would hold true through the weekend, or at least for the fondue party tomorrow night, since it was planned to be on the patio at the winery. The last thing I needed was for us to get washed out. The thought of being stuck in close quarters with these folks and a bunch of bubbling pots was not one bit appealing.

I checked my phone for the time and realized I still had nearly two hours before I was due back at the Lancaster house.

"Come on, Cocoa," I told the dog, deciding to sneak him around to the side door through the kitchen and into Aunt Meg's room. Nobody would even know he was there if they didn't see us. The two of us headed around the side of the house, Cocoa happily trotting behind me. When I got to the kitchen, I stuck my head in and surveyed the territory, then motioned for him to follow me inside. I could hear Barry and Kevin arguing in the front room still and took it as a sign that the coast was clear.

"Okay, bud. Let's go." We snuck down the hall and made it to Aunt Meg's room without a fuss. I turned on the tv and found a rerun of Matlock, which Cocoa seemed to enjoy. He hopped up on the bed and I sat next to him and gave him a pet. It really bugged me that he was being discriminated against, but there wasn't a thing I could do about it. I hung out with him for a few minutes and gave him some love before I left him to his own devices. "Be good now. I'll be back soon. No barking."

He panted at me, and I could swear he was giving me a smile. I smiled back, gave him one last chin scratch and then headed back out to the front room to see what fresh trouble might be brewing.

Chapter Six

Heading back out to the front room to hang with Aunt Meg and Bertie a while longer before I needed to leave, I was happy to find the room free of guests for the time being. Luckily there hadn't been any more drama in my absence and we settled in for more catching up, Aunt Meg and Bertie with a glass of white wine and me with an iced tea since I'd need to go back to work shortly.

Eventually, I looked at my watch and sighed. "Time for me to get a move on. Cocoa's in your room for now. I would take him home, but Cassie's having a date night and I don't want to interrupt. I'll take him home after I pick up the catering stuff. Sorry he caused so much trouble. I'll keep him out of sight until the guests are gone."

Aunt Meg patted my leg, and Bertie lifted her brows. "Ooh, a date night! You didn't tell me Cassie is seeing someone!"

Bertie settled back into the couch and sipped her wine as Aunt Meg filled her in on Cassie's dating life. I knew the talk would turn to Ryan as soon as I walked out the door. Waving to them both, I skedaddled, wanting to get away quickly so I wouldn't get pulled into any more conversation and be late for the catering pickup. But my ears were burning as I headed out to my car.

Sugar Creek was quiet as I made my way across town in the Connolys' van. A few bars and restaurants on Main Street were hopping, but the residential areas were buttoned up and mostly dark for the night. I slowed down as I spied a raccoon family on the side of the road. It was a good reminder that all sorts of nocturnal critters were out doing their business now that most of the town was in for the night. Many a car wreck happened at this time of night when white-tailed deer and cars tangled on the road.

There were still a couple of cars parked on the street near the Lancaster home when I pulled up to the ranch-style house a few minutes later. I grabbed a box with to-go containers from the back of the van and headed inside. I couldn't leave my equipment and mess at their house overnight, but I could at least leave the lingering guests all the leftover food.

I knocked before stepping inside. Most of the party was still out n the yard, but I found Mr. and Mrs. Lancaster in the kitchen talking to a friend. I hated to interrupt, but I had to get the job completed and get back home.

"Hey, there, y'all. Sorry to just walk in. I knocked, but there wasn't an answer. Figured the party was still in full swing."

"Oh! Abby!" Mrs. Lancaster cried as she turned to me. "This is the caterer I was telling you about," she told her friend as she swooped over to give me a quick hug. "The food was magical! It made the night so lovely for us. Everyone couldn't stop talking about it! And eating it!" she said with a laugh. "Thank you for all the hard work you've done."

"And that cake," Mr. Lancaster rolled his eyes back in his head and patted his stomach. "That was something else."

Mrs. Lancaster laughed and leaned into her husband. "The grandkids sure loved it. I might have to get the recipe from you, although I'm not sure I could pull it off half as nice as you did.

Normally, I don't like having much sugar in the house. But Tom is right, it was so delicious! And we *are* celebrating, after all."

"We certainly are," Mr. Lancaster said, rubbing her back. "I still can't believe you put up with me for fifty years. That is definitely something to celebrate."

We all laughed as I pulled out the containers and started piling up leftovers. "I'm sorry I have to pack my things up, but I'll leave all the food behind."

They thanked me profusely and handed me an envelope as I packed up my equipment and did a last scan for anything left behind. I blushed and stuck it in my back pocket. The money aspect of my job was still uncomfortable for me, especially when clients gave me tips. I was so used to cooking for the joy alone that it still felt strange to charge people money for my food. Thinking about how badly I needed to buy myself a catering van helped me to make my peace with it, though.

Most of the lights of Primrose House were out by the time I got back to the B&B, but I saw a few still blazing, including in the dining room, which wasn't a surprise. I had no doubt that at least one workaholic was still burning the midnight oil. I cut the engine and glanced at all my equipment in the back with a sigh. It was so tempting to just leave it for the morning. But I knew I needed to get the van back to the winery early, and I didn't want to have to unload everything in a rush the following morning, so I grabbed a chafing dish and headed around toward the kitchen door.

As I edged around the side of the house, I realized people were over on the other side of the big live oak and they were whispering. My heart pounded, and I stilled, not wanting to be seen. The hushed whispers floating in the air sent a chill down my spine, and I crouched near the bushes. The last few months of sleuthing and near misses with killers had fine-tuned my senses to any hint of danger, and right now, they were screaming warnings at me. I crouched low, my breath catching in my throat, as flashes of recent troubles flickered through my mind. Peering cautiously, I prepared for the worst, only to spot the familiar silhouettes of Barry and Tori beneath the moonlit branches. Relief mingled with a surge of curiosity as I realized they were not merely enjoying the Texas night air. Their bodies pressed against one another in a way that could only mean one thing.

Tori's voice, laced with urgency, broke through the still night. "Barry, think about it. Once we get this sale over with, we could... we could take everything and vanish. Just the two of us."

There was a pause, the air heavy with unspoken things. Barry shifted away from her uneasily, his silhouette outlined against the dim glow of the garden lights. "Tori, it's too much. I've poured my life into this company. You can't imagine what I've done to make all of this work. So many sacrifices. So many risks. Walking away like that..." His voice trailed off, fraught with conflict.

"But imagine it," Tori pressed, leaning in closer, her hand grabbing his as if to physically pull him into her plan. "No more board meetings, no more deadlines. No more Kevin trying to tell us what to do. We could be free, Barry. Completely free. The amount of money we're talking about, we'd never have to work again."

Another pause hung between them, filled with the buzz of night bugs and rustling of leaves. Barry seemed to waver, the temptation tangible in the air. He whispered something to her I couldn't make out, and I frowned, debating between sneaking closer and getting the heck out of dodge. Not wanting to be caught in the act of spying on guests, I regretfully but quietly backed away. As much as I wanted to know what they were talking about, I had a responsibility and I knew Aunt Meg wouldn't appreciate me jeopardizing the B&B's reputation for a piece of juicy gossip. I'm not sure why I wanted to know so badly, although curiosity was clearly a problem for me, as evidenced by all the spying I'd done since I'd returned to Sugar Creek.

Straightening slowly, I turned and made my way to the front of the house, deciding to go through the lobby instead. As I did, I noticed a curtain move back into place in one of the upstairs bedrooms. Looked like I wasn't the only one eavesdropping on Barry and Tori's rendezvous. I wondered who else might be spying on the couple.

A side lamp that Aunt Meg always left burning in the front room lit my path to the kitchen and I placed the chafing dish on the rack where it lived and sighed, leaning against the counter, letting the adrenaline rush of catching Barry and Tori recede. At first I'd been afraid there was some sort of intruder, but the fear had quickly turned to the fear of being caught snooping. I took a deep breath, suddenly exhausted, and decided that the rest of the unpacking could wait until the next morning after all.

I didn't want to disturb Aunt Meg, but I needed to get Cocoa and take him home with me. Creeping down the hall, I was relieved to find a light on under her door. I knocked quietly. "It's Abby."

"Come on in!"

Cocoa bounced around me as I came through the door. Aunt Meg was sitting up in bed reading with a cup of tea.

"How'd things go with the Lancasters?"

"Great," I replied, and remembered the envelope I'd stuffed into my jeans. I stood and pulled it out and tears sprang to my eyes as I opened it, feeling overwhelmed by the amount of cash that was in my hands. So many people in Sugar Creek had come together to help my business succeed, and I would be grateful forever. I looked up to find Aunt Meg watching me with a small smile.

I smiled back. "How was the rest of your night with Bertie?"

Aunt Meg sighed and frowned, looking down at the teacup in her hands. "We didn't get much time together, unfortunately. The California bunch came in wanting to order takeout and weren't happy with what Sugar Creek has to offer. I ended up driving over to Fredericksburg to pick them up Thai food and Bertie stayed here to make sure they didn't burn the house down or kill each other while I was gone."

"I'm so sorry, Aunt Meg. I don't know why they couldn't have gone out themselves."

"They fought about it for a while," she said with another sigh. "I can't imagine having to work with them day in and day out. That Cheryl woman has largely stayed in her room since they got here, I noticed. I don't blame her a bit. I'd try to hide if I was her, too. The rest of them have been a near constant struggle."

"I'm sorry I wasn't here to help. Tomorrow I'll stick around as much as I can. I have some shopping to do for the dinner party, but otherwise I should be free to help...for a while at least."

"It's okay, honey. You've got a business of your own to run, I know that." She put her cup down and frowned, lying back on the pillows. Her eyes were puffy, and she looked worn to the bone. "I *did* get to talk to Bertie a little more about her life on the beach. It sounds lovely. You know she walks two miles a day? She has a book group and goes out to dinner with friends." There was longing in her voice and I ached for her, suddenly realizing how much she gave up to run Primrose House. I knew she enjoyed it most of the time, but it had to weigh on her that she didn't have the same freedom that Bertie had. Especially when she had to deal with troublesome guests like the ones she had now.

"You know what you should do? You should take the day off tomorrow. I'll come over early and take care of everything, at least until I have to leave for the dinner party. You should go pamper yourself with Bertie." I hesitated about what to say next, but she looked so tired and so down. "It was supposed to be a surprise, but I booked a spa day for you and Bertie for Tuesday. I'm going to call in the morning and see if they can fit you in tomorrow instead."

Her eyes brightened, but then she frowned. "I couldn't do that, honey. Tomorrow is a big day for you with the dinner party and everything. I'm sure you'll have your hands full."

I shook my head. "It's no big deal. Maria will be here too, right? Between the two of us, we should have everything under control. And if there's any emergency, I can always call you back.

It's not like you're going on a road trip or anything. Trust me, I've got this."

She fretted, but I waved her protests away. "I won't hear another word. I'll call in the morning and see if we can get you in."

She grabbed my hand and gave it a squeeze. "You're too good to me, you know that?"

I leaned over and gave her a hug. "Nonsense. You took Devon and me in when Mom and Dad died. I'll never be done repaying you for all you've done for me."

Before she could make any more protests, I stood and patted my leg for Cocoa to follow. He hopped down after a quick stretch and wagged his tail. I said goodnight before gently closing the door and then worried about her all the way out to the car. I knew the current group was a handful, but it wasn't like her to be so negative, so out of energy. My stomach churned at the thought of the double work and the possibility of disaster I was putting on myself for the following morning, but I knew I needed to give Aunt Meg this gift. She needed a break and needed one sooner rather than later.

CHAPTER SEVEN

The next morning, after I'd gotten dressed, I was sipping a quick cup of coffee and trying to make a shopping list when the doorbell rang. Cassie was still in her room, so I followed Cocoa's wagging tail to answer it. The way he danced and yipped, I knew it was someone I wanted to see.

I grinned wide when I opened the door to find the most gorgeous man I'd ever seen standing there with a bouquet of wildflowers in his hand. Ryan Iverson's thick dark curls were still slightly damp and he wore his sheriff's uniform. He gave me a smile that melted me and handed me the flowers.

"I only have a few minutes before I need to be over at the station," he told me as he stepped inside, stooping to pet Cocoa's head. "But I really needed to get a look at you in person, if only for a minute."

He stood and pulled me to him, kissing me so deep I felt it all the way to my toes. It made me want to throw all my plans away, to grab this man and drive off into the sunset. But life had other plans for the both of us, for today at least.

"Thanks," I said as we finally parted lips. I nuzzled into his neck and we hugged each other for a moment. "I've missed you."

Between his work and mine, we didn't get to spend time together in person nearly as much as either of us would have liked. We talked on the phone and texted often, but it wasn't the same thing as having the real Ryan in my arms.

"I've missed you too. Sorry it's been so crazy. Losing Arnie really stretched us thin." One of the Sugar Creek deputies had recently died of a heart attack, and the entire station had taken it hard. I knew it wasn't just a staffing issue that they were struggling with. The group of them were like family and they'd lost one of their own.

I rubbed his arm and moved to the kitchen to find a vase for the flowers. "It's okay. I know things are hard for y'all right now. After this event I'm doing tonight, I have nothing else on the books, so I'll be a lot more free soon. I could even come over to the station and hang out sometime. I mean, if that's not too weird. Or illegal." I flushed, knowing that the legality of an activity had never been much of a barrier for me before. And knowing that Ryan knew that too made me blush even deeper.

He laughed. "Sure. I'm interviewing a few new candidates for Arnie's job next week, but otherwise we shouldn't be too busy. I should have more time off, too."

I leaned into him and put my head on his chest. Closing my eyes, I inhaled deep, hoping against hope that the scent of him and the feel of his powerful arms around me would linger after he left. We spent a few more minutes talking and then he said goodbye with a long kiss that both of us were unhappy to pull away from.

I hit the stores as soon as I dared. I had a pile of shopping and cooking to do for the fondue party and I wanted to get it all taken care of quick since I'd promised Aunt Meg the night before that I'd take over the B&B tasks as well. Because it was early Saturday morning, there weren't many people out yet, and I rejoiced at the empty streets as I made my way down the block from Cassie's place to my first stop, Sugar Creek Bakery, to visit my friend Ellie. I needed a variety of breads to cube up for fondue dipping, and only Ellie's bread would do.

"Hey, there, Abby! How's my favorite chef?" Ellie called from the counter. It was early enough that I'd beat the morning rush and the shop was empty save for me.

"Not too bad. How's my favorite baker?"

Ellie laughed and beamed at me. Her cheeks were flushed and there was a twinkle in her eye. If you looked up "morning person" in the dictionary, there would be a picture of Ellie Baxter. But I supposed that came with the territory of keeping baker's hours.

"I'm fantastic," she told me as I got to the counter. The smile on her face bordered on ecstatic, and I wondered what I was missing. Surely she wasn't this happy all the time.

"What's going on? Is it your birthday?"

She laughed. "Nope."

"Did Garett win the lottery? Please tell me you'll keep the bakery even if he won the lottery."

"Nope, not that either."

"What's going on, woman? Tell me already!"

She leaned over and whispered, "I'm pregnant."

We both squealed. I knew Ellie had been trying to get pregnant for a long time and the news overjoyed me.

"It's a little early still, but the doctor says things look good. And I simply can't keep it to myself any longer. Besides, knowing you, you would have figured it out even if I hadn't told you. What with those sleuthing skills and all."

I laughed and then leaned over the counter and pulled her into a quick hug. "I'm so happy for you! Garett must be crazy excited!"

"He is," she said, but her voice changed, and she grabbed a rag and started wiping down the counter.

"But..." I prodded.

"But..." she looked back up at me and sighed and then crossed her arms over her chest. "He wants me to stop working. He's worried it'll be too much, that it might hurt the baby if I work such long hours at a physical job."

My heart ached for Ellie, knowing how much the bakery meant to her, but also knowing how important having a family was to the two of them. "I'm sorry. I know that must be difficult. Could you hire more help, maybe?"

She nodded slowly and fiddled with the string on her apron. "That's what I'm looking into. It'll make our margins pretty tight. But it's better than selling the bakery. That's the last thing I want to do."

I squeezed her hand.

"Boy, that is a tough situation. I'm sorry, Ellie. If I can do anything to help, just let me know. But also, what an exciting problem to have!" I gave her hand another squeeze, and she smiled back at me, absolutely glowing. She touched her still flat stomach.

"You're right. Whatever ends up happening, it's all for the best. I'm sure I'll be able to work things out. And once this little guy or gal is in the world, who knows what might change? It's just hard for me not to fret. Okay, so you're obviously not here today to comfort me," she said with a laugh. "What can I get you?"

Giving her hand one last squeeze, I said, "I'm so happy you told me. I feel honored to know. And you better let me cater your baby shower!"

"You know I will!"

My face turned serious, and I examined some of the delicious looking sugary goodness in her front case. "I'm doing a fondue party tonight, a small one. But I'll need some bread for dipping. Something sturdy that will hold up well in the cheese."

"Yum! You're making me hungry, girl!" She moved to a rack by the far wall and scanned it for a moment, then grabbed two loaves and headed back to me. "Sourdough is a no-brainer. Nice and thick, it'll hold up no problem and it's got enough of a taste that it won't get lost in a cheese sauce. The other option I have is a little more intense. This is my dark rye. It's a recipe from

Garrett's German grandma. It's delicious, but it's not for everybody."

"I think I'll take one of each. They both look beautiful and I like to have some variety. I was also thinking about some sort of cake for the chocolate fondue if you have it. Again, something kind of sturdy but not overly heavy, if that's possible."

Ellie smiled and pulled out a tray from the case loaded with thick slabs of airy angel food cake. She took the top slice and cut a piece off, handing it to me. "What do you think about this?"

It was like a sweet vanilla cloud in my mouth and I closed my eyes as I savored the treat. "Yes, that is exactly what I was hoping for," I said, as I finished chewing. "I think I'm going to have to take the rest of that slice to go," I told her with a laugh.

She laughed too. "Glad you like it." It only took her a moment to wrap the breads and a full angel food loaf for me and ring me up. In the meantime, I'd managed to snack my way through the rest of the angel food slice she'd given me.

Wiping my hands on my pants, I pulled out my business credit card. It was still an exciting new feeling, putting things on my business card. It made me nervous spending money, but I really enjoyed it too. Something about the "Deep in the Heart Catering" printed on the front of the card always lifted my spirits and made me proud.

"Good luck tonight," Ellie told me as she handed me the breads. "Come by sometime next week and let's sit down and chat."

"Will do! And congrats again. I'm so happy for you!" I said it with a little squeal, which she returned.

I left Sugar Creek Bakery with a smile on my face. It was a beautiful Saturday morning—a little hot, but the birds were singing—and I could smell jasmine blooming nearby. The rest of my errands blew by in a daze, my mind busy with plans for the party and Ellie's news. Midway through my shopping, I made a quick call to the spa and got them to move up Aunt Meg's appointment. Finally, after finishing everything I needed to get done, I headed over to Primrose House, feeling very proud of myself.

The streets of our little town whispered of the day's slow awakening, but I knew the calm wouldn't last. The closer I got to the B&B, the more my anticipation grew of what I knew would be a bustling day ahead. Once I turned onto the farm road leading to Primrose House, my pulse picked up the pace. It was a surprise to realize I wasn't looking forward to the day's catering work. Usually kitchen work soothed me. But worries about the group and my decision to serve fondue despite my misgivings kept all the joy at bay. Grey dust kicked up in the parking lot as I turned in and I let it and my nerves settle a moment before opening the door of my Honda.

I took a deep breath and grabbed some grocery bags, prepared to go to battle.

Chapter Eight

Primrose House was the height of calm when I stepped into the kitchen a few minutes later and I breathed a sigh of relief as I started putting the food away. Morning sun filtered through the window over the sink and lit up the butcher block island where I did most of my cooking when I worked at Primrose House. The kitchen was like an old friend to me. I'd grown up learning to cook in this very room and now and then, flashes of the past still came back to me, warming me with their comfort as I worked.

I was unpacking all the vegetables when Aunt Meg came in. Grinning at her, my eyes went wide. "Aunt Meg! I called the spa and they're happy to take you and Bertie today. So be off with you, woman! Go do some relaxing. I've got things covered here."

Bertie came in just then, and she gave a little whoop when she heard what I said. She was bright eyed and full of energy, decked out in a sunny flowered tank top and shorts. She looked ready for an adventure. But Aunt Meg looked worried. "I don't know, Abby. I don't feel comfortable leaving..."

I shooed her words away with a wave of my hand. "Don't even think about saying no! I am totally capable of handling a few fussy

Californians for the day. Besides, Maria is here to help. You deserve this, Aunt Meg. You've worked so hard for so long. Please. If you don't do it for yourself, do it for me and Bertie."

Bertie grinned and nodded. "That's right, and for your business too! Taking a day to yourself will refresh you. Give you the steam you need to keep moving forward." She leaned into Aunt Meg with a friendly nudge. "Or you could do it for me, if you're so bent on being selfless. Keep me company, Meggie! I'm lonely!" She made a sad face and batted her eyes, and we both laughed.

"Okay, okay! Jeez! I can see it's pointless to protest. Let me go get my bag together."

As she left the kitchen, Maria came in. "Good morning, Abby!"

"Maria! Just the woman I wanted to see! I'm sending Aunt Meg to take a day off with Bertie, so you and I are on B&B duty. If you have any problems, come to me rather than Aunt Meg."

"No problem," she said with a smile. She moved to the coffee and tea station to restock after the morning crowd and Bertie sat at the counter. As they did, I got things organized for a day of cooking, setting out my cutting board and sharpening a couple of knives.

"Hey, I was wondering," I said a moment later, "what upstairs room looks out into the side yard? The one with the window on that side," I said and pointed.

Maria frowned and thought for a moment. "I believe that is room six."

"Who's staying in that room this week?"

"I believe it's Mr. Warren...Kevin? Why do you ask?"

"Well, I was bringing things back from the job last night and a funny thing happened." I hesitated, not sure I wanted to spread gossip, but also knowing I couldn't help myself. "Barry and Tori were out in the yard together. They were...close. And they were talking about something possibly illegal. And I noticed that someone in that window was watching them."

Maria raised her eyebrows. "Ooh, some intrigue. This sounds exciting!"

Before I got any further, the couple from California came into the kitchen. "Sorry to interrupt. We were just looking for some coffee."

"Help yourself, Maria just made a fresh pot! Are you enjoying your stay so far?" I asked them as I pulled out a massive hunk of Gruyere to grate. I would grate all the cheeses for the fondue and toss them with almond flour and nutmeg. Much as I hated to substitute the usual corn flour I would have used, I couldn't call the dish keto otherwise. The flour helped the cheese to melt smoothly rather than clump and I knew from experience it was essential to a good cheese fondue. I only hoped that the almond flour could do the same work for my sauce.

"Yeah, there aren't as many amenities as we're used to, but the traffic is great. Sure beats being stuck on the Bay Bridge, right, hon?"

"Oh, I thought you said you were from San Diego. I was in Los Angeles for a while, so I know California fairly well," I explained.

The couple passed a quick look between them. "We *are* from San Diego, but we have family in the Bay Area and visit there a lot," the woman said as she stirred cream into her coffee. "Sometimes it just feels like we live there," she finished with a laugh and sipped her coffee.

I gave them a smile. "Do you have any plans for the day?"

"We were planning to do a little sightseeing around, visit some wineries. Might check out the one down the road later on."

"That sounds great. There are so many good places to visit around here. Hope you enjoy your day!" I gave them a wave and a smile as they headed out.

Aunt Meg came back a minute later with her bag packed and a flowy sundress on. She looked lighter already, and it thrilled me I'd be able to play a part in giving her a break.

"Alright, you better call me if you need anything at all. I'll keep my phone on. Don't hesitate, I'll be back in a jiffy…"

"Aunt Meg! Stop fussing and go have some fun!" I said with a laugh.

She pulled me into a hug and pat my arm. "Good luck today, honey. We'll see you after the dinner party gets through."

"Have fun!" Maria and I waved them off. "I'm going to clean the rooms, but when I'm done, I'd be happy to help with the food if you need me to," Maria told me.

I nodded and smiled as I chopped through a head of broccoli. Maria had been a great help to me in the kitchen on several occasions. Although I felt like I had this event under control, which was a good thing because the two of us had a B&B to manage now, too. Throwing the broccoli into boiling salted water, I quickly got a big bowl of ice water and set it by the stove, then grabbed a straining spoon. I planned to blanch a variety of vegetables that would be delicious in both the cheese and broth fondues, of which the broccoli was the first.

I like to take my time in the kitchen. Many chefs like to be known for their speed with a knife, but if I could swing it, I really enjoyed slowing down and making everything just right. Don't get me wrong, if it was important to haul butt, I certainly could. I'd learned to work a kitchen line like a pro and chop an onion or carrot to perfection in seconds. But the genuine joy for me came when I slowed down a little and I was happy I had plenty of time today before the dinner party to enjoy the process.

Midmorning, Maria came in wringing her hands, her eyes wide with anxiety. "Abby, I think you should come. The group, they are trying to move things around in the dining room. They said they want to change it for a conference call."

I wiped my hands on my apron and turned the stove burner off with a frown, then followed her down the hall toward the dining room. The sound of scraping and arguing floated out of the open door.

"Hey, y'all, is there something I can help you with?" I scanned the room, trying to hold the shock from my face as I took in the mess they'd already made. The collection of vintage teacups, candlesticks, jewelry boxes and potted plants that had once graced the room's bookshelves littered one half of the dining table. A spread of computers, keyboards, and camera equipment spread out over the other half. Kevin and Eric were busy trying to move a bookshelf that held a variety of fiction we stocked for guests to enjoy during their stay. The books leaned precariously one way and then the next, about to fall out.

"We've got it. Just need to make this look..." Kevin stammered as he turned red with effort, "...more professional."

As the words left his mouth, a pile of books finally tottered too much and fell out of the shelf, crashing onto the table on top of the trinkets. A breaking clash jarred my nerves, and I frowned as I hurried over to see what they'd broken. Eric and Kevin barely noticed the trouble they'd caused as they dropped the bookshelf on the other side of the room, revealing a bare wall behind that was a shade lighter than the rest of the paint in the room. Those bookshelves had been in place for as long as I could remember.

I scanned the items, carefully stacking books as I went. It took me a moment, but I finally found the item that had broken and my heart sank.

A beautiful porcelain vase with a Japanese scene painted in gold and shades of blue lay in pieces all over the table. The vase was a gift Uncle Nolan had given Aunt Meg after his last trip overseas. I knew it was something she deeply cherished.

"Sorry about that," Cheryl murmured as she watched me scoop up the pieces, but there wasn't much regret in her voice. She'd already turned back to the computer screen before I could respond. I sighed and tried to keep the tears from my eyes as I left the room. The damage was already done and I couldn't see how I could either help them or keep them from causing any more damage than they already had.

"Well, it probably didn't cost much. This stuff is all junk anyway," I heard Tori say as I left the room. The tears I'd been holding back surfaced when I heard her comment.

Just like that, I was done with these people. It wasn't the fact that they'd broken the precious vase, but the callousness with which they'd done it. The rudeness and lack of concern for others was too much. I had a job to do for them and I would do it to the best of my ability, but I wouldn't spend one more second trying to win them over or convince them of the charms of Texas. I would get in and get out, and good riddance when they finally left.

"That is a shame," Maria said, bringing a box to me for the pieces as I headed back into the kitchen. "They are not very considerate."

The tears had gone, but my heart still hurt. "Uncle Nolan gave this to Aunt Meg right before he died. It was very precious to her. She's going to be heartbroken when she finds out."

She patted me on the back and I gently set the box of broken pieces on the kitchen table. "Is it possible to fix it?" she asked.

I shook my head. "It's in a million pieces. I can't imagine any way it could get fixed."

"You never know," Maria said with a small smile, a thought crossing her mind. "Do you mind if I take it? I might know a way..."

I nodded. "I got all the pieces I could find, but some of them were tiny. Don't worry about it too much."

She smiled and shrugged. "We'll see. And now I am sorry to have to leave you, but I need to get home to Daniela. I could come back with her if you want..."

"No, don't worry about it. I have things under control here. I don't think it could get much worse, to be honest. We only have a little longer before we're heading over to the winery, anyway. Thanks for your help today. Say hi to Daniela for me."

She took the box of broken pieces and waved goodbye. I could tell she was torn about leaving me, but I shooed her away and she finally headed out.

I spent the rest of the afternoon trying hard to ignore the chaos of the group. They could do what they wanted with the room. Maria and I would put it back to rights once the upset of their presence had passed. Well, as closely as possible at least. I turned all my attention to the dinner party, trying hard not to think about who I was making the delicious meal for.

I'd started a chicken bone broth in a massive pot earlier that morning and I dipped a spoon into the simmering liquid to check the taste. It was rich and full of flavor from the herbs, garlic, and vegetables I'd added with the roasted chicken. It would need a bit of a kick if I was going to call it fondue, but I planned to strain it and then add in a variety of seasonings, more garlic, and wine at the table and let it bubble a little longer before the party got started.

The work proved to be a balm after all as I organized the variety of fresh and blanched vegetables, seafood, sausage, bread, and fruit for the dipping station I planned to set up. Getting everything finally ready, I looked at the clock and noticed with a grateful sigh that it was nearly time to go over to Wild Hare Winery. The sooner I got this job finished and got back home, the better.

Bertie and Aunt Meg still hadn't returned by the time I got everything for the dinner party prepped and packed, so I put together a surprise fondue kit for them and tucked it away in my catering fridge with instructions on how to make it. I left one of the vintage fondue pots—a bright orange one—in the center of the counter where they wouldn't miss it, with a note for them to look in my catering fridge for a gift. Then I headed out to my car, ready for anything.

Or so I thought.

Chapter Nine

Ten minutes later, I was out in the parking lot, packing my tiny Honda with all the food for the party, when Mark Connoly pulled into the lot in his vintage green VW bus and honked. Cheryl was on the front porch, phone in hand, and she stepped inside to get the rest of her crew, who followed her out to the lot. For once, they seemed like they were in the mood for a party. I wondered if whatever they'd been working on had turned out a success.

"Hop on in, folks!" Mark called out as he pulled up to the porch and opened the sliding door for the group. Every one of them hesitated, looking at the worn VW bus with deep skepticism.

"It's safe, I swear it!" He said with a laugh.

The younger man, Eric, was the first to climb in. I was happy that he'd finally left his laptop behind. Cheryl followed him next, throwing a quick, unsure glance back at the house.

"I'm going to call an Uber," Tori growled from the top of the stairs as she pulled her phone out of her designer purse and scowled at the old van.

Kevin groaned. Barry frowned at her. "Get in the van, Tori. You're being ridiculous. It's a two-minute drive."

She scowled at him and then when she realized everyone else was glaring at her, she gingerly went down the steps and climbed into the bus without touching a thing as if terrified some of the age or the hippy vibes might rub off on her.

"Cool van, man," Barry said as he climbed in after her.

"Thanks," Mark replied with a grin as he stepped around to the driver's seat. I knew how much pride he felt for the old bus and I caught his eye and gave him a smile.

"I'll be right behind you," I told him as I leaned in the open passenger window. "Just have a few more things to pack up."

"No problem, Abby. See ya in a few. Alright folks, buckle up!" Mark said with a chuckle as Kevin settled in, and then he shook his head with a big belly laugh. "Just kidding, this old girl doesn't have seatbelts!" I heard a few protests as he quickly pulled out of the parking lot and I breathed a sigh of relief. At least we got them out of the B&B. But I doubted they would climb back in that van to come home. I'd probably end up giving them all rides.

Or, who knew, maybe they would call themselves an Uber.

I followed a few minutes later with all the pots and pans and utensils and food that I thought I might need to feed a fussy party of five for the evening. Everything rattled as I made my way down the dirt road that turned off the main farm road the winery shared with Primrose House and my car sputtered a few times as if protesting the load.

Wild Hare Winery was one of the prettiest properties in Sugar Creek. The main house and yard sat on the top of a hill overlooking rolling waves of grapevines and the occasional oak tree. The front of the house was your average farm type arrangement, with a wrap-around porch, spindle topped alcoves, and a screen door on the front of the house. But Sheila and Mark had spent decades reworking the place to be a destination spot for tourists. The porch on the front changed to an incredible stone outcropping of a patio on the back of the house with a couple of big wood awnings covered in dusty purple wisteria, a deck rail made of old grape vine wood, and several tables where customers could sit and enjoy the wine and the view.

Surprisingly, there weren't many other people at the winery for a Saturday afternoon. It was a hot one, but I would have thought more people would have made their way to such a lovely destination. A few other patrons carried their glasses among the vines or hung out at the bar near the front of the house, but otherwise our group had the place to ourselves.

As I brought food around the porch to the back where the party would be, I noticed that the other couple from the B&B were at the winery, too. The two of them huddled close together, sharing a bottle of white, holding hands and looking out over the vista. I was glad they were enjoying their trip and that they were giving our friends some business.

The California group mingled on the patio as Sheila poured them each a glass of Wild Hare's signature Pinot Grigio, and talked about the wine that she and Mark had lovingly made by hand and had perfected over decades of owning their winery. The group seemed lighter here away from their laptops and I tried hard to give them some grace despite all the trouble they'd caused. I truly hoped they would enjoy their evening away from their work. With glasses of wine in hand, they seemed removed from the high-stakes world they inhabited, their conversation a blend of relaxed banter and the occasional tech jargon that felt only slightly out of place among the vineyards.

After Sheila got the group squared away, she came over to say hi.

"Wow, this looks great, Abby," she said as she watched me melt the chocolate chunks with cream in a dark green fondue pot at the end of the table. "It would make an impressive spread for wine tastings. Maybe someday soon we can put something together. We could do the wine and you could do the food."

"I'd love that!" I told her with a smile. Glancing to the west, I frowned. "Hopefully, the weather will hold tonight. I would hate for their dinner to get ruined."

"I checked the weather before y'all got here," Sheila told me, "and it looks like we will get some thunderstorms, but not until later tonight. They should all be back at Primrose House by the time it hits."

I breathed out a deep sigh as I piled the cubes of sourdough and rye bread onto a platter. I looked over my shoulder to see where the group was and then leaned in. "Between you and me, I hope these people behave for you tonight. They've been quite a handful for us. They broke something of Aunt Meg's and didn't even apologize earlier." I couldn't keep the frustration out of my voice.

She tsked and rubbed my arm. "That's too bad," she replied. "With any luck, a little of our delicious wine will ease the tension."

I nodded, and she patted me on the back. "Come over next week and we can talk about doing that tasting together."

"That would be wonderful." It was a great idea and helped me to make peace with myself over the decision to serve fondue this evening. Even if the Californians ended up not liking the dinner, it looked like it would lead to a new job for my catering company, which was definitely a bonus. I stirred the cheese and the chocolate to make sure they were melting properly, turned the burner up a little under the broth, piled fondue forks in the center of the table, and then I called everyone over.

"I'm sure you've all had fondue before, so I won't spend a lot of time explaining," I told them as they settled into their seats with their wine. Mark moved silently around and put new bottles of red and white on the table as I talked. "I've made a classic Swiss fondue, a chicken broth fondue, and a chocolate fondue for dessert. There's a variety of things to dip. And the broth and cheese are both keto friendly. Everything is vegetarian except for the broth and the shrimp. Let me know if you have any questions. I hope y'all enjoy your dinner."

I stood to the side near one of the wisteria awnings and watched as the group began piling their plates and dipping things into the bubbling pots. Happily, it seemed like they were enjoying everything. I breathed a sigh of relief. Only a few more hours and I would be off duty with these people. I couldn't wait.

I hung out with Mark and Sheila for a while as the group enjoyed their dinner and caught up with them. They'd been in my life since I was a child, and I was always glad when I had time to gab with them. I paused from time to time to walk around the table, making sure the fondue was still the right temperature and restocking anything that was running low. As the group ate and talked, bottles of wine littered the table and voices grew louder, but in a boisterous, friendly way.

Eventually, the group finished their dinner and got up to enjoy the views, so I moved in to clean up the mess, eyeing the growing dark clouds with concern. The storm seemed to move toward us much more quickly than it had earlier. At least I'd gotten everyone fed before the party got washed out.

Out of the corner of my eye, I noticed that Barry and Tori had drifted away from the rest of their group, wine glasses in hand, into a shadowed alcove of the vineyard. Their body language was tense, a sharp contrast to the relaxed ambiance of the patio. I tried to focus on my culinary duties, but the undertone of their voices, laced with urgency and frustration, was hard for me to ignore and I picked up snatches as I piled plates and forks up.

"You've got to let this go," Barry growled and threw back the rest of his wine.

Tori started to protest, but he rudely walked away from her and the hurt showed all over her face. But it only stayed there a second, shifting from hurt to anger to a blank stare in a blink of an eye. She caught me looking and glared at me. Flushing scarlet, I spun back to the food on the table and began stacking the leftover bread into Tupperware.

A few minutes later, I was packing up the dirty dishes in a box near the house when Cheryl came over to me with a smile. "Thank you for that dinner. It was lovely," she said. "I was skeptical when you suggested fondue, but I think everyone enjoyed it very much."

"Oh! Thank you. I'm so glad to hear it," I said with a smile. It was nice that at least one of them had the decency to thank me.

"Do you know where the bathroom is, by any chance?"

I pointed to the side of the house. "Just through that door and to your right."

She smiled and glanced back at the group on the patio, then went toward the side door I'd pointed out. I finished packing the dishes into my box, but before I had time to carry it to the car, a scream pierced the air, high-pitched and filled with terror. The evening's calm shattered like the fragile wine glass that now lay in pieces on the stone patio at Tori's feet. Tori and a few others stood next to a broken rail of the patio, looking down at the drop to the ground.

"Oh my God, Barry!" she shrieked, her voice laced with panic. She trembled and her hands clasped over her mouth.

I rushed over to look down and saw Barry Golding lying on his back on the rocky ground below, no sign of life. The CEO of NexTech Dynamics was dead.

Chapter Ten

I called Ryan immediately. "You need to come out to Wild Hare and bring an ambulance. Someone has died. He fell off the patio."

"You sure he's dead?" he asked me.

I frowned as I looked at the body that hadn't moved. Blood seeped into the ground behind his head. "Pretty sure."

My eyes darted around all the people on the patio. Some winery visitors were staring down at the dead man, others clustered in small groups, talking quietly. The California group all stood at the rail looking down at their dead boss. All except Cheryl, who had come back from the bathroom sometime in the last couple of minutes. She stood off to the side with her hand to her mouth and tears in her eyes. The B&B couple still sat at the table they'd been at all night, their faces hard to read through the sunglasses they both wore.

As I watched the lot of them, I texted Aunt Meg. I figured she needed a warning about what was going on. No doubt it would be a long night for Primrose House.

Something's happened. We might come back early. Barry is dead.

She responded after a minute. *Are you kidding? What's going on? Do you need me to come over?*

No, I replied. *Barry fell over the ledge of the patio and Ryan is on his way. I'll let you know when we're heading back.*

I kept my distance from the ledge, not wanting to get another glimpse of the body, but also not wanting the Californians to realize I was observing them. Glancing down at the broken railing, I noticed that rather than looking like it had snapped with Barry's weight, the bar looked like it had simply pulled away from the post, as if nothing had held it in place to begin with. I would have to point that out to Ryan when he arrived. I hoped it wasn't something that would lead to trouble for Mark and Sheila.

Eric and Kevin were arguing, but it was too loud on the patio to hear what they said to each other. Tori was obviously in shock. I moved back to the table and started cleaning up the dipping station as I waited. Between the death and the increasing rumbles of thunder, this party was definitely coming to a close, and the sooner I put things away, the better it would be for me.

Less than ten minutes later, Ryan pulled up with two deputies and an ambulance only a minute behind. He surveyed the patio, looked down at Barry a moment, walked around the place, and then walked over to me.

A flurry of voices erupted as the guests crowded around the compromised railing to watch as two EMTs with a stretcher picked their way over the rocky terrain below toward the body.

"Hey, what happened?" he asked me quietly.

Frowning, I told him about hearing Barry go over the ledge. "I didn't see it myself. I was cleaning up after dinner and heard Tori yell. When I came over here, it looked like he was already dead."

Ryan placed his hands on his hips and frowned. I couldn't believe we were once again discussing someone's death. What I wanted to do was grab him and hold on tight. What I wanted to do was feel the comfort of his protective embrace. Instead, I wrapped my arms around myself, knowing he would comfort me later. Right now, he had a job to do.

The group of Barry's coworkers crowded around Ryan a moment later, eager to share their own tale.

"I don't think it was an accident, sir," Kevin began. "Barry was arguing with Tori just before this, wasn't he, Eric? I saw them. I think you did too." Kevin said, frowning quickly toward Eric and then casting a sidelong glance at the visibly shaken woman.

"I didn't push him!" Tori cried as Ryan turned his attention to the group. "That's what you all think. I know it!" Her eyes darted quickly around it her coworkers. "But I didn't do it! I'm not sure how he fell. Maybe he had too much to drink?"

Ryan turned to her. "You were standing with him when he went over the edge, Ma'am?" he asked.

She shook her head and then nodded. "I'm not sure. It all happened so fast! I'm very confused. We were talking, and there were other people around us too. Close to us. I looked out to the clouds because I heard a rumble, and just like that, he was gone."

Eric's face turned sour, and he said under his breath, "maybe if you weren't so focused on talking to him all the time, people wouldn't think you pushed him."

Tori's eyes slanted into slits, and she stared him down. "Stay out of it, Eric! You're just jealous. Everybody knows it."

Eric let out a laugh. "Are you kidding me? Jealous of that guy? I don't think so."

As Ryan talked to them, I headed over to Mark and Sheila where they stood to the side.

"I think something is wrong with the rail," I whispered to Mark. "Look at that railing. It's not broken at all. That shouldn't have given way, not the way it did. It's almost like it's been unscrewed or something. Have you noticed anything loose or damaged lately?"

"No! Not at all! Oh, no!" Sheila cried. "I don't know when we had someone out here last to do a thorough inspection. I sure hope it isn't our fault."

"I don't think it's your fault. What I wonder is…" my voice trailed off as I scanned the group of Barry's coworkers.

Sheila followed my gaze. "You think somebody messed with it?"

I raised my eyebrows. "It's possible. But maybe I'm just looking for trouble where there is none. You know me, always thinking somebody's been murdered," I said with an uncomfortable laugh.

I jumped about ten feet when a voice very close behind me said, "Let me guess. You're already sleuthing."

I twisted around and gave Ryan a friendly smack on the arm. "Don't scare me like that, mister!"

He crossed his arms over his sculpted chest and I couldn't help but get momentarily sidetracked by the thought of those arms wrapping around me. I closed my eyes and took a deep breath, willing myself to concentrate on the problem at hand.

"I'm not sleuthing. I'm just observant."

Ryan nodded toward the broken railing. "You noticed it's been tampered with too?"

I nodded, happy to have my suspicions confirmed. "Looks like somebody loosened the screws or took them out all together. I don't know, what do you think?"

Ryan frowned. "That's what I thought too. It was meant to look like an accident, a man who'd had too much wine falling off a balcony at a winery. It would be a good coverup. But yes, I think something is off in this whole scenario. The question is, which one of them could be responsible?"

Before anyone said another word, a deep rumble erupted from the sky and my stomach turned as I realized we were about to get hit with a massive storm. The wind kicked up and leaves blew around the patio erratically. Glancing around at the food and service items still scattered around, I realized I needed to get things put away quickly or I'd get caught in the middle of the downpour, cleaning up food, which sounded like a nightmare.

Ryan turned back to the Californians but before he could ask any more questions, Cheryl interrupted.

"I'm sorry, but it feels really unsafe out here right now," she said as a crack of lightning illuminated the sky, making her point for her.

She jumped. "Can we do this somewhere else?"

Ryan nodded and looked around. "How'd y'all get here?" he asked.

Mark held up his hand. "I drove them."

"Would you mind taking them back to Primrose House for me?"

"No problem, Sheriff."

Ryan glanced at me. I was hustling, trying to collect all my supplies. His gaze moved between the catering equipment and food I was frantically packing up and the group of murder suspects standing around, then over to the ambulance taking care of Barry's body. I could see the pain all over his face. He wanted so badly to help me, but he had a job to do himself.

"It's okay," I mouthed, giving him the warmest smile I could manage under the current chaos.

He frowned, but nodded. "Alright, folks, let's get you back to the B&B and we can talk more there. Hey, Charlie! Call me when you get to the coroner!" Ryan yelled down to the EMT.

"Sure thing, Sheriff," the young man replied.

I looked around to find the other couple from the B&B to see if they needed a ride back as well, but didn't see them anywhere. They must have left on their own after Barry died. Right now, it didn't matter, though. I needed to get everything packed up and back to Primrose House before I got washed out completely.

Chapter Eleven

It began to pour right before I got the last of the food packed up in my car. Luckily, the rest of the group had already started back, and the EMTs had finished their gruesome work by the time the sky opened up. The storm lashed out wildly at my car as I headed back to Primrose House, and I could barely see through the rain to the road in front of me.

As I crawled along, trying to avoid the quickly overflowing ditches, I thought about everything that had happened. The rail at the winery had definitely seemed tampered with. I scanned my memory of the evening, trying to remember if anyone had spent an unusual amount of time there, but nothing stood out. It was also possible that someone had visited the winery some other time and messed with the rail before our party, but whatever the answer, clearly someone had gone out of their way to make that spot dangerous. The way Tori had made it sound, Barry might've just been drunk and lost his balance. But that's what the rail was there for. No, someone had banked on the idea that he would get drunk and fall. Or be pushed. But if that were true, how would they have known that Barry would be the one to fall to his death and not someone else?

Someone had likely pushed him. Someone like Tori? The way she'd acted so confused about what had happened didn't ring true to me. She wasn't the type to get so flustered, at least not from what I had seen over the last few days. She'd been arguing with him only moments before and it wouldn't surprise me one bit if she had pushed him to his death.

But several other people had been there next to the broken rail as well. It could've been any of them. If Tori knew she was under suspicion, why wouldn't she have told Ryan straight away if she'd seen someone else push him, though? It was all very confusing.

Once I pulled into the parking lot of Primrose House, I sat in the car for a minute, trying to decide what to do with all the food and equipment from the fondue party. The last thing I wanted was to traipse in and out of the B&B in a torrential downpour. What little food was left wouldn't be good anymore anyway, since the group had picked it over, so I left it all. Droplets hammered down like a relentless drumbeat as I sat looking at the B&B. Sheets of water blurred the familiar outlines of Aunt Meg's cozy haven, turning it into a hazy silhouette against the stormy night, and I hesitated a moment longer, not ready to deal with the madness that was surely happening inside.

Finally, I gritted my teeth and ducked my head, running as fast as I could in the slippery mud toward the front porch. I entered the house with a bang of the door, the wind nearly knocking it out of my hands, and found the Californian group along with Ryan, Ty, Aunt Meg and Bertie, all in the front room staring each other down.

The California group huddled together, their faces reflecting shock, grief, and unspoken fears. I noticed that someone had opened a bottle of wine and they all had a glass.

"Abby, you're soaked through! Let me get you a towel," Aunt Meg said and jumped up before I'd taken more than a couple of steps inside.

"Thanks, Aunt Meg," I replied. I stood where I was, dripping onto the carpet until she returned and handed me a fluffy cream colored oversized towel. The room had grown quiet with my arrival and everyone eyed me warily. I dried myself off quickly and then moved to the couch where Bertie and Aunt Meg sat and perched on the arm closest to Bertie.

"Meg, I'm going to have Ty search Barry's room. Would you mind showing him the way?" Ryan asked.

Aunt Meg nodded and hopped up again, pulling out her master key ring. Ty followed her up the stairs, and Ryan turned to the rest of the group. "I'd like to speak with each of you individually for a few minutes. Who would like to go first?"

Kevin's arm shot up and he stood from the wingback chair he'd been lounging in. "I need to get back to work, so if we could make it quick, that'd be great." There was no concern or remorse in his voice and his callousness shocked me. His boss had just died a horrible, unexpected death and Kevin seemed like he couldn't care less. It made me wonder what his role in Barry's death might be.

Once they headed down the hall toward the dining room, the others eyed one another with suspicion, the silence between them continuing to echo through the room. Eric pulled out his phone and scrolled and Tori bit her lip and looked out the window. Cheryl fiddled with a button on her shirt.

I leaned over to Bertie and whispered, "sorry we had to cut your night short. How was the spa?"

Her face lit up. "We had a wonderful time," she said. She squeezed my knee. "And thanks for the fondue. We had ourselves quite the fancy meal. I'm happy I'm getting the chance to meet your new boyfriend, even if it is under unfortunate circumstances. Woo, what a looker! And so sure of himself. He seems like quite the catch."

I blushed bright red. "He *is* pretty fantastic, although it's very new. I don't even know if we're at the boyfriend-girlfriend stage exactly. But we're on our way somewhere, at least," I said with a laugh.

"Oh, that man is smitten with you. I could see it all over his face as soon as you traipsed in like a drowned rat." We both laughed and then she continued. "It's a shame that the night had to come to such an awful close, though."

I nodded. It really was a shame. The dinner party had gone so well, I was starting to think we might be on the other side of the troubles from the group. But clearly that was nothing more than a pipe dream.

Aunt Meg returned from upstairs and snuggled back in between Bertie and me. My face turned grim. "Did you see the dining room, by any chance?" I wondered if she'd realized the extent of the damage the group had done before we'd left.

Aunt Meg's sad eyes said it all. "I did. I'm sure there's a story there, but I'm not sure I want to hear it."

"Not one worth talking about. I'm so sorry, but they broke the vase Uncle Nolan gave you."

She gave me a sad smile and squeezed my hand. "It's not your fault, honey. It's a shame. But it's not one bit your fault."

After we chatted quietly for a while longer, Ryan returned, followed by a frowning Kevin. "Alright, who's next?" he asked the group.

With a long, overly dramatic sigh, Tori stood. "Might as well get this over with."

She followed him down the hall and Kevin sat down next to Eric, pulling out his phone as well. Cheryl tapped her foot and twirled her hair around her finger, her eyes darting everywhere around the room.

It was strange to me that none of them were talking to each other. If it was me, I'd want to commiserate with the others who'd known the person who'd died. But that didn't seem to be the case here. These people seemed totally disconnected from one another and it made me wonder just how hated Barry really was. What a sad way to live. I couldn't imagine having so little concern for my coworkers.

Aunt Meg, Bertie, and I continued to murmur in the corner as we all waited for Ryan to finish his interviews. I thought about moving into the kitchen, maybe making a snack for everyone, but I hated the thought of missing anything and I knew the others felt the same. So we all stayed and watched and waited, as one by one Ryan spoke to each person in the group.

After what seemed forever, Ryan came back into the room. "Thank you all for your cooperation. We'll work our hardest to get this figured out quickly. I know this is a difficult time and I know y'all are far from home, but I'm going to have to ask you to not leave town until I give you the okay," he said, his tone gentle yet firm.

There was a collective groan, and then everyone grew silent. No one's eyes met. The rain continued its relentless symphony, a backdrop to the unfolding drama. The sound seemed to underscore the tension, each droplet a reminder of the fragility of the situation. Ryan shot me a look and gestured his head for me to follow him.

I hopped up and followed him to the kitchen, and he gave me a warm smile as I came into the room. He didn't come over to me though, and I got the message that he was still in sheriff mode.

"I guess I'm done here for the night. We should probably talk a little more about what you saw tonight, but I can stop by in the morning. I know you've got your hands full with work and you're probably dead on your feet. But is there anything you want to tell me right away that seems important?"

Leaning against the counter, I wrapped my arms around myself. "I don't know if it means anything, but I overheard a few things between Barry and Tori that might be important."

He arched an eyebrow and moved over to rest against the same counter, then leaned into me. It was subtle, unnoticeable to most anyone, but I flashed with excitement at his touch. His scent was so close and so comforting. I desperately wished that we were alone. Leaning into him slightly too, I told him about seeing Barry and Tori together the night before, and about what I'd overheard from them both last night and this evening before Barry died.

Ryan frowned. "Good. That's exactly the kind of thing I need to know."

My cheeks flushed. I was happy I could be helpful. Lord knew I had created enough trouble for him over the last months with my snooping.

"You think it means something?"

He shrugged. "It all means something. What I need to figure out is what?" He pushed himself from the counter and gave me a grin, then took my hand quickly and kissed it. "I don't know if I'll be able to do anything fun tomorrow like I promised. Depends a lot on how all this plays out. But I'll call you in the morning. And I'll probably be stopping by here again for follow-ups, so maybe I'll see you then if you're around. I'm sorry you're dealing with all this death business again. Kind of hard to believe."

My heart went out to him and I squeezed his big palm hard, then pulled him into a quick hug and kissed his cheek. "I'm sorry *you* are going through it again. You moved to Sugar Creek to get away from this kind of craziness and here you are right back in the thick of it."

His eyes darted to the kitchen doorway and then he snuck a quick kiss before pulling away. "It's okay. It's my job. And trust me, this is still a far cry from the violence we dealt with in Dallas." A deep sadness crossed his face, but only for a moment before he gave me a sweet smile. "Sleep tight, honey. We'll figure it all out, don't worry."

As he turned to go, I grabbed his powerful hand, giving it one last squeeze, not ready to say goodbye.

"You might want to talk to the other couple staying here too," I told him. "They were at the winery tonight as well. They were already gone by the time you got there, but they may have seen something that would help."

Ryan nodded and squeezed my hand back, then left the kitchen. I immediately felt the tug of his absence. He was so good at calming my worries, of making me feel safe. I wished, not for the first time, that we could be together all the time. But that was a big step, one that seemed outrageous to be contemplating only a couple of months after we started dating. I wondered, did he feel the same way? Only time would tell, I supposed.

Chapter Twelve

After Ryan left, I spent a few minutes alone looking out the kitchen window at the blustering storm. Ryan had told the group they couldn't leave until he gave the okay. I wondered how long we would be stuck with these people. And I wondered how willing they would be to continue to pay for their rooms even though they were being asked to stay by the police. I hoped it didn't lead to any more trouble for Aunt Meg. She was already up to her eyeballs in trouble, and this was an added complication.

It was so frustrating and sad that all of this had to happen at all, but even more frustrating that it had to happen when I'd worked so hard to make Aunt Meg's birthday special. I frowned, my stomach flip-flopping as it occurred to me that these people might be stuck here even through the day of Aunt Meg's birthday party. I'd made my plans assuming we would have the house to ourselves. If the guests were still here, it would ruin everything. I knew she would feel obligated to work and to involve them too. It was too much for me to think about at the moment.

I sighed deeply. What a mess.

A few minutes later, I went back out into the front room. The group still huddled there, sharing yet another bottle of wine. Two empty bottles sat on a nearby end table.

"I can't believe this is happening," Kevin cried as he drank deeply from his glass. "Barry dying is going to wreck the bid to go public. There's no way it'll happen with this kind of scandal hanging over our heads."

"I thought you wanted control," Tori said with a sour look. She sipped her wine and said coldly, "why don't you just take over as CEO? In fact, maybe you killed him so you could get control. From what I remember, you were as close to him on that patio as I was when he fell."

He lunged at her and raised his hand like he was going to slap her. Eric immediately dove between them.

"Hey. Stop. I know tensions are tight right now. We were all under a ton of pressure anyway, and this just blasted things to epic proportions. But sniping at each other isn't going to do any good."

"Give me a break with the good boy act, Eric. For all we know, it was you."

"What?" Eric said with a frown. "What are you talking about? Why would I..."

"We all know you have the hots for Tori," Kevin spat out. At this, Tori rolled her eyes.

I wanted to get popcorn, the drama was so thick in the room. Aunt Meg, Bertie, and I watched as the group dug into one another. Cheryl got up and wandered down the hall.

Eric flushed scarlet. "That isn't true. And besides, even if it was, I wouldn't kill Barry. He was like a father to me," he said as tears sprang up. I wondered if they were real or only an act. It was so hard to tell.

Kevin rolled his eyes and knocked back the rest of his wine. "You and I both know there was a heap of jealousy going on. Tori was sleeping with Barry, and you wanted Tori. That's enough of a reason to kill, in my book. Happens all the time. Isn't it almost always about love and jealousy?"

Tori growled then. "I was not sleeping with Barry."

They both gave her skeptical looks, and she almost crumpled. She drank deeply from her glass and paced. "Fine, maybe I was. But it has nothing to do with anything that's happening now."

I headed back to the kitchen to brew some coffee. All the wine was getting to people's heads. The last thing we needed was for the group to start fighting.

Walking into the kitchen, I found Cheryl leaning against the counter, biting her lip and texting furiously. She jumped when she noticed me and stuck the phone in her pocket.

"Oh, sorry to interrupt. I'm going to make some coffee if you want any."

She frowned. "Uh, yeah, sure. Coffee. Sounds good."

I measured out the beans and glanced at her. I could tell she was itchy to pull her phone out again. "Are you doing okay? I know it's been a hard day for you all."

Cheryl's hands shook, and her eyes darted around the room. Her face was a mixture of sadness and something else. Fear maybe? I realized as I watched her pace the kitchen that she was the only one of the group who seemed to be mourning Barry in any way. "It's just... Barry's death...it doesn't make sense," she murmured, almost to herself more than to me.

I paused, the coffee maker sputtering in the background, filling the silence. "It's a terrible shock for everyone," I said, attempting to offer comfort.

She nodded, her gaze distant. "You know, Barry had his faults, but he didn't deserve this. He was a ruthless man. He had no problem making enemies, doing underhanded things to get his way. Barry always had to have his way." She shrugged. "But I guess that's how CEOs are, right? I guess a person can't really lead a company without being hardheaded. So many people hated him. This was bound to happen, eventually. But I can't help but feel responsible." Her voice trailed off, laden with an emotion I couldn't quite place—guilt, perhaps, or sorrow.

That caught my attention. "Responsible? Why would you feel that way?"

Cheryl hesitated, then sighed and shook her head. "Sorry, that wasn't the right word…We all had our disagreements, like any close group does. The decision we were trying to make… it was getting to everyone, fraying nerves. It was my idea to come out here to Texas. I thought getting out of the constant insanity of our regular office would do us all some good, ease the tension around the decision. But now Barry is dead."

"What was the decision y'all were trying to make, if you don't mind my asking?"

"Kevin wanted to take our company public. Barry wanted to sell it to a small private firm from India. The two of them were constantly fighting about it, and whatever they decided would affect everyone at the company, so it was really important that they make the right decision."

Before I could probe further, she quickly changed the subject. "But what's done is done. I just hope we can all find some peace after this." She forced a smile, but her eyes didn't match the sentiment.

As she accepted the cup I offered her, her phone buzzed in her pocket. She pulled it out and glanced at it, then quickly silenced it. "Sorry, just… family stuff," she said, though her expression suggested it was serious. "I've got to go handle this. Thanks for the coffee."

Cheryl sipped as she scanned her phone and then left the room quickly, without another word.

Grabbing a tray, I added a few mugs, cream and sugar, and the coffee carafe, and headed back into the front room. The group was still arguing amongst themselves, louder and more drunkenly than before. Aunt Meg and Bertie were gone. No doubt they'd had enough of the chaos. After putting the coffee next to them, I retreated to the kitchen once again, as fast as a duck on a June bug.

I poured myself a cup of black and puzzled over the exchange with Cheryl. What would she have to feel responsible about? And what did the decision to go public or not have to do with Barry's death, if anything at all?

A few minutes later, Aunt Meg and Bertie came in. "Well, this has been some night," Bertie said and let out a long breath.

"It's enough to make a person want to quit this business," Aunt Meg said with a sigh.

"No, Aunt Meg. Don't think that. I know this is really difficult, but you can't let it get you down. This thing will get worked out. Ryan will figure it out quickly. And then these people will leave and we'll go back to having regular, simple, lovely guests. I'm sure of it."

She sighed and moved to make herself a cup of peppermint tea. "You're right. It's been a long day, that's all."

"We've been around this crew more than anyone else in town. Certainly more than the police. Is there anything the three of us could do to help Ryan out? Anything we could share with him that might speed things along?" Bertie asked.

Aunt Meg shot her a look of horror, but only for a second. I could tell she was thinking about how she didn't want me to start sleuthing again. But this time, it was more personal. This time, a killer had come into her home to stay and wouldn't be allowed to leave until the mystery was solved.

"We need to be careful, girls. Whoever killed Mr. Golding is in this house. There is no doubt in my mind. And the more we snoop around, the more danger it brings. To all of us," Aunt Meg warned, staring at me as she said it. I got the message loud and clear. She'd never been a fan of me digging into murder before, and she wasn't about to support it now.

"You're right, it's dangerous. Which is another reason to get this thing figured out and get them out of here, pronto. Bertie's right, we have more access to these people than anyone else. I think it's time for us to start paying a whole lot more attention. We don't need to do anything that would make them notice, but we can certainly keep our eyes and ears out for trouble. For instance, when I was coming back from the catering job last night, I overheard Tori and Barry in the side yard. They were whispering about some plan after they sold the business, something about... taking the money and disappearing together. I told Ryan and he said he would look into it, but that's just the kind of thing I'm talking about. We could probably find out all sorts of tidbits by just staying observant."

Bertie's eyebrows shot up. "Disappearing together? That sounds like a motive for something underhanded. And with Barry now dead..."

I looked out the kitchen window into the storm that showed no sign of letting up. Rain smacked against the pane. "It seems on the surface like Tori is a good suspect. But why would she kill him when she'd been trying to convince him to run away with her? The impression I got is that she was in love with him, not that she wanted him dead. Although the way she looked at him earlier this evening when they were arguing..." I shivered, remembering her steely glare when he'd walked away from her. "I don't know."

"That's a good point, if she was really in love with him. Unfortunately, there isn't much way of knowing. That kid, Eric, could have done it out of jealousy, like the other one said."

I nodded. "Or Kevin could have done it because of the business stuff. Cheryl told me a little, but it's mighty confusing to me."

"What about Cheryl?" Aunt Meg asked. "Any thoughts about her role or whether she might have a reason to want her boss dead?"

"She seems to be pretty upset about it all. I don't think it was her. She doesn't seem the type. Besides, she was in the bathroom when he fell. I remember that clearly."

Bertie shrugged and looked out the kitchen door toward the front room. "Well, there has to be one actual answer. And I think it behooves us to keep an eye on things around here. A careful eye on things," she added as she squeezed Aunt Meg's arm.

Aunt Meg sipped her tea and frowned. "Please promise me that neither of you will put yourself in harm's way just to figure this out. I know how you get," she said, eyeing me.

Crossing my finger over my chest, I promised. "I'll be careful. And I won't do anything crazy."

Aunt Meg raised her eyebrows and her mouth quirked up in a smile. "If you're gonna make that kind of promise, you might also need to promise not to tell Cassie."

It was true. I loved my best friend, but she sure had a knack for getting us into trouble. Still, there was no way I was keeping all of this from her. I dodged Aunt Meg's comment as I set my empty cup into the kitchen sink. "Did the other couple make it back? I didn't see them at the winery when I left."

Aunt Meg nodded. "They got home a little before you all came back."

"That's good," I replied. "I should probably get going pretty soon. I have a lot of the catering stuff to put away, but I think I'll save it for the morning. Hopefully, the weather'll clear up by then."

Bertie said goodnight and gave me a quick hug and then I leaned into Aunt Meg for a hug as well. She seemed so frail tonight. So much concern was etched on her face.

"Do you want me to stay tonight?" I asked her. "I could help make sure the guests are all taken care of. Help out if there's any trouble. They're in a funny mood. I'm not sure I trust them."

She shook her head. "Thank you, honey, but I've got it for tonight at least."

"Okay, but you better call me if you need anything at all. I don't care what time it is. I'll be back in the morning." Giving her one more quick hug, I steeled myself before heading out into the blustery night.

Chapter Thirteen

Cassie was already in bed by the time I got home, so I waited to fill her in the next morning. Because it was Sunday, she didn't have to open her shop until noon. I busied myself with making a pot of coffee and refilling Cocoa's food and water bowl while I anxiously waited for her to get up. I couldn't wait to share the news.

"You will not believe the night I had," I told her as soon as she emerged from her room, her hair a tangled halo of blonde curls and her eyes bleary.

She moved automatically to the coffeepot and poured herself a cup.

"Let me guess, somebody got murdered."

A look of shock crossed my face, and then turned to disappointment. "You already talked to Ty."

Her eyes went wide. "No! I was just making a joke! Are you serious?"

I nodded and stroked Cocoa's belly absently, and then I was struck by a thick guilt, remembering Aunt Meg's warning the night before about Cassie getting us into trouble. Oh well, there was nothing to be done about it. Cassie and I were so close, there was no way I'd keep it from her. "Barry, the CEO of the California group. He fell over a broken rail at the winery and died."

Her hand shot to her mouth as she processed what I'd told her. "How do you know it wasn't an accident?" she asked as she slid onto a barstool and sipped her coffee.

"Someone tampered with the rail where he fell, took the screws out, or something like that. Ryan saw it and he agrees. Someone murdered Barry. And everyone in their group is up in arms toward each other, throwing blame every which way. I hope Aunt Meg is holding up okay with all the craziness. Speaking of which, I should get over there soon," I told her as I finished my coffee, stood, and stretched.

"Hey, if you'll wait a few minutes, I'll go with you. I haven't even gotten to see Bertie yet!"

"Sure, no problem." I went to my room and perused my closet, wanting to look good but effortless, too. Knowing that Ryan planned to stop by, I chose a cute linen shirtdress and sandals, then put some makeup on.

A few minutes later, as we were gathering our things to leave, Cassie said, "Hey, I know what we should do! Let's invite Ryan and Ty over for a nice home-cooked meal. Even if they're working, they need to eat, right? Maybe we can weasel some information out of them." She rubbed her hands together. A regular villain. I laughed, but then frowned and bit my lip.

I was torn. I really wanted to know what Ryan and Ty had found out so far. The faster they figured out who killed Barry Golding, the faster we could send the California people on their way. But I was also wary of getting involved in yet another murder investigation, especially if Ryan didn't want us meddling. The budding relationship between us was much more important to me now that things had picked up for real, and I hated the thought of messing it all up because I couldn't keep my nose out of his investigations.

"I guess so. I don't know that they'll tell us anything." My mind immediately turned to ideas for what to cook. Thinking about getting to spend time with Ryan again and cooking for him made me smile. "But I guess it doesn't matter too much either way. It would be fun, right?"

"That's right," she said. "I'll text Ty a little later. Or if we see Ryan at the B&B, we can ask him."

I nodded and grinned, suddenly excited at the possibilities. We had the whole day ahead of us and I had no plans other than to keep Aunt Meg and Bertie company. There would be plenty of time to cook whatever I could dream up, and I was in the mood to impress my new man.

"Alright, let's head over to Primrose House to see if there's been any fresh developments. Besides, I haven't even gotten to see Bertie yet! I need my Bertie fix!" Cassie declared.

I laughed and nodded. I was itchy to check on Aunt Meg after all that had happened.

"Can Cocoa come with us, you think?"

I glanced at the dog, who sat with one ear cocked, watching us. He gave me a look that was as close to a grin as a dog could get, like he was promising me he'd be on his best behavior. I was tempted, especially now that Barry was no longer with us and couldn't complain. But I had a feeling someone else in the group would pitch a fit about an animal presence. "Best if we don't," I replied. "Sorry, buddy."

I gave him a chew on the way out the door and he took it over to his bed in the corner, resigned to being left behind once again.

Opening my car door, I immediately regretted not taking care of the catering things the night before. The warm morning air that wafted out was stale with old food and nearly made me gag. "Uh, sorry about the smell," I told Cassie as she opened the passenger door.

She coughed and waved her hand in front of her face. "Good grief, lady! What is that?"

"Old cheese," I told her and couldn't help but laugh at the

absurdity of it all. "I left the stuff from the dinner party overnight. It was storming like crazy last night and I thought it would be fine to wait. Guess I was wrong."

"You wanna take my truck instead?" She gave me a pleading look, but I shook my head.

"Sorry, but I've got to get all this over to Primrose House and take care of it. You can take your truck if you want and follow."

She slid into the passenger seat and rolled the window down. "It's fine."

Luckily, it was a short drive, and it was early enough that the breeze flowing in through the windows was pleasant rather than stifling. After only a minute, the smell faded, but I seriously dreaded doing the dishes once we got to the B&B. I made a note to myself: *never again wait to take care of things after a job.*

When we arrived at Primrose House ten minutes later, Cassie and I each grabbed a box of dirty party dishes and headed into the house. I braced myself as we headed up the porch, wondering what we might find when we entered.

But the house was quiet and clean, no sign of the mess from the group's powwow the night before. Maria gave me a warm smile as we came in. "Abby, Cassie! Good morning! Do you need help with that?"

I shook my head. "I've got it, but thanks for the offer!"

Her eyebrows rose. "Sheriff Iverson is here. He's interviewing the couple."

I flushed and grinned, giddy that I would get to see him again so soon.

"Oh! Good!" Cassie said over her shoulder as she headed back to the kitchen with my catering equipment. "Now you can invite him to dinner."

I frowned, still not sure the dinner was a great idea, as I followed her down the hall. "I've got the rest, thanks, Cass," I told her as I slid my box of dirty dishes onto the counter near the sink.

When I opened the dishwasher, I was grateful to find it empty. I had several loads to do.

Cassie went off to find Bertie, and I headed back to the car to get the rest of the things. As I made my way up the porch steps on my last trip, Ryan pushed the screen door open for me. I grinned at him and nearly shivered as I passed. He smelled like fresh linen and masculine aftershave. "Well, hello there, Mister Iverson."

He took the box from my hands and, after throwing a quick glance behind him to the empty room, bent down for a kiss. I knew how important it was for him to be seen as professional and in charge, especially when in uniform around a group of murder suspects. I blushed and kissed him back, and then we headed to the kitchen.

As I scrubbed pots and loaded the dishwasher, I talked to Ryan.

"Anything new about Barry? That you want to share, I mean," I said with a blush. "I'm not snooping, I swear! Just making conversation."

He laughed and then his face turned serious. "We found a few things, actually. They're doing some background checks on the business and all the employees over at the station. A few things have come up..." he hesitated and looked around his shoulder to the entryway leading to the front room and shrugged. "But we can talk about it later..."

Before we got any further, Cassie came into the kitchen with Bertie. Cassie's eyes lit up.

"Hey, Ryan! Hi! Abby has something to ask you! Don't you Abby?"

I rolled my eyes. I loved her to death, but sometimes she didn't know when to stop. "We were wondering if you and Ty would like to come over for dinner tonight."

"Are you cooking?" he asked, his eyes dancing and his lip turned up in a smirk.

"You know it."

He crossed his arms over his chest and leaned back onto the counter. "Is this just a clever ploy? Why do I get the feeling that y'all are trying to weasel info about the murder out of us? You know it won't work."

Cassie's smile was sly and sweeter than stolen honey. "Now, Ryan. Why would we do something like that? We're just missing our men, is all."

Boy, she could lay it on thick when she wanted to.

He threw his head back and laughed out loud. "Okay, sure. As long as we don't have any emergencies, we should be able to swing it. But Ty is on call tonight, so he'll have to be ready to leave at the drop of a hat."

Cassie beamed at me, and I struggled to keep a smile from my face.

"We'll take it. Maybe around seven?"

"Sounds good. I'll let Ty know when I get back to the station." He sighed. "Alright, I've got to get going, but I'll see you later tonight. Unless something comes up."

"Oh, hang on a sec," she told him and turned to me. "You planning on staying a while, Abby?"

I nodded. "Probably a few more hours, at least." I wanted to check on Aunt Meg and help her as much as I could.

"Would you mind zipping me back home real quick? I need to open the shop soon," she asked Ryan.

"I can take you back, if you don't mind riding in the cruiser."

Cassie's eyes lit up. "Do I get to sit in the front this time?"

He laughed. "As long as you promise not to touch anything."

She nodded, and I chuckled when I saw her fingers crossed behind her back. That girl sure loved trouble.

I followed her and Ryan to the front room and gave him a long hug before saying goodbye to them both.

"I'll see you later tonight, unless something comes up." He dipped his head and gave me a peck on the lips.

Cassie gave me a quick hug and then ran through the parking

lot after Ryan with as much energy as a pack of squirrels. I could just imagine the ride she and Ryan were about to have. It made me giggle to myself.

After they left, I turned to Aunt Meg, who was standing behind the desk in the corner, and gave her a smile. But before we even had a chance to say hi to each other, the couple from California came into the front room, wheeling their bags behind them.

"I'm sorry, but we've decided to check out today instead of Tuesday," the man said, setting his key down on the desk.

"Oh, no! I'm sorry to hear that. I hope there was nothing wrong with your stay at Primrose House," Aunt Meg told them.

He shook his head. "No, nothing like that. It's just..." he paused, shot his wife a glance. "We've decided to spend the last part of our vacation in Austin. We've never been."

Aunt Meg tried hard to keep the disappointment from her face, but I could tell it hurt.

"I understand," she told him and moved to the counter to print him out a receipt and process his payment.

I left to go find Bertie since Aunt Meg was occupied. I wanted to talk to her about the birthday without Aunt Meg around to protest. It was time to make some positive plans and to get things back on track around here. Aunt Meg was going to need the best party we could create to help pull her out of the mood she was in, and I planned on giving her just that.

Chapter Fourteen

First, I headed outside to think for a few minutes. I'd only been at Primrose House for a little while but already I was feeling overwhelmed by the negativity and drama and I hadn't even had any run-ins with the business group yet.

I paced slowly near the flower beds with my arms crossed, letting the buzzing of the bees and flitting of busy butterflies capture my attention for a while. It was hot, but beautiful out. No sign of the massive storm from the night before other than a few piles of leaves and a stray downed branch here and there.

It was a shame that the couple was leaving early. My guess was that they were tired of being surrounded by drama from the other group and wanted to enjoy themselves somewhere drama-free, which made plenty of sense to me. But it was too bad for Aunt Meg's business. What a shame that the group was continuing to cause us problems. I wondered if there was any way I could help on the money front. I knew finances were already tight without the cancellation, but with no catering jobs on the horizon, there wasn't much I could do either. Bookings were solid during weekends for the rest of the month, but with school right around the corner, business for Aunt Meg would drop sharply. If only I could get a few more jobs lined up, I might be able to help out with the money some. I kicked a pebble thinking about it, but I was at a loss on how to get more work. I'd tried everything I could think of.

Right as I was heading inside to find Bertie, she came outside and found me. "Abby! Good, just the woman I was looking for," she said, her eyes dancing.

I gave her a big smile. "Ready to talk about birthday plans?"

She nodded, and I motioned to the picnic table that sat under the shade of the live oak. She followed me over through the still-wet grass.

I pulled my hair back and tied it in a quick bun, knowing it wouldn't take long for the heat to make me sweat. "I don't know what to do now that the California people are probably still going to be here," I told her. "My original plan was to do a big potluck over here on Tuesday night. Cassie even got one of her friends who has a band to agree to play for a couple of hours for free."

"That sounds fantastic. You know what? We can still do all that with that group here. It's a B&B, not a nursery. They can find their own entertainment for the evening."

"My worry is that they'll decide to crash *our* evening. Things haven't exactly been smooth with them around."

Bertie frowned. "Is there another option?"

"We could wait until they leave. But I know you've got to go home, eventually. And who knows how long they'll be here? We could try to have it somewhere else, but I'm not sure where. Cassie's place is too small. And I don't want to put anyone else out asking for that big of a favor."

Bertie shook her head. "No, that wouldn't do. This is the right place to have her party. And you're right, I need to get going before too much longer, although I can stay at least a couple days longer than I'd planned. It's not like anyone is waiting for me..." her voice trailed off and she looked into the distance, a momentary pain crossing her face. She shook it off and smiled at me again. "You know what? We need to keep our plans. We can't let these people, with their silly requests and their drama, destroy our fun. They'll just have to work around it. And if they don't like that, they can go stay somewhere else."

She was right. We were bending over backward, trying to work around people who couldn't care less about us. I nodded. "You're right. Let's keep it here on Tuesday night. We've got the band coming at seven. We can serve food around six so people will be free to dance if the mood takes them. I was hoping sometime Tuesday you could get her out of the house so Maria and I can decorate. I'd planned for y'all to be at the spa, but I had to pull that up yesterday."

"No problem, honey! I'm sure I can find all sorts of trouble for us to get into."

I laughed. "Just not too much trouble. You'll need to have her back in party spirit by five."

"You have my word," she told me. She grinned and gazed around the yard. "It sure is pretty here. You happy to be back from L.A.?"

I nodded. "I'm so much happier. Things are slower, friendlier. It's nice to have Cassie...and Ryan." I blushed and carried on. "And I love having my own business! There's no way I could afford something like what I'm doing out in L.A. I'd have to pay an arm and a leg for kitchen space and supplies. Not to mention the insane amount of competition I'd face," I finished with a shudder.

"It all sounds so exciting! How amazing that you own your own business! I bet it keeps you so busy."

I laughed. "Not as much as I'd like at present. But I'll get there."

"I'm sure you will, doll. Truth to tell, I'm a little envious." She sighed and gazed out again at the field behind us. "I'm not sure what I'll do once I go back to Spoonbill Bay. The last few weeks since I left Rick have been very relaxing. But I'm already getting bored, and it worries me. I've never been without something to do, either raising kids, cooking and cleaning, or teaching. There was always something going on. I love to read, but there's only so much sitting on my bum that I can handle before I get stir-crazy."

"I know just what you mean. Catering can be exhausting and it's always stressful when I'm not making enough money. But boring is one thing it never is. Every job is different, every day in the kitchen is different. I love it." But right now, as worried as I was about the lack of money and future jobs, I didn't know if I'd be crazy enough to keep going if it wasn't for the love of it all. At present, I was one hundred percent fueled by passion.

I sighed and glanced around the yard too, catching sight of Kevin, who walked out the door with a cell phone on his ear. "What do you make of all the hoopla around this murder?" I asked Bertie as I watched Kevin walk into the side yard and pace.

"It's tricky. That's no lie. Could be any of them, I suppose. It seems like the blonde girl is guilty, but I don't know, it also seems like that's a little too easy. Or maybe I've just watched too many of those crime shows," she said with a laugh.

Kevin moved closer, and we both stopped talking, whether to not have him overhear our conversation or so that we could overhear his, I wasn't sure. He was almost whispering, although he was close enough now that we could hear every word, but the frustration in his voice was clear as day.

"This is it, the moment we've been waiting for," he muttered, stopping mid-stride as if to emphasize his point to the person on the other end. "Barry's gone, and it's time to shift gears. We can't afford to waste this chance. I've got plans, big changes that need to happen. I want to move forward on taking NexTech public."

Kevin stopped talking to listen, and the pacing resumed, a physical manifestation of his restless ambition. "Yes, I know it's sudden, but we need to act fast. Barry's death... it's unfortunate, but it opens doors for us, for the company. We need to move quickly, reposition ourselves. I'm ready to lead, to take us in a new direction."

I lifted my eyebrows at Bertie, a look she returned.

His voice dropped, almost conspiratorial, "Barry held us back too long. I'm stepping up. It's my time." Kevin's determination was palpable, his intentions cloaked in ambition.

Bertie and I stared at each other as we listened to Kevin talking. I tilted my head in his direction, wanting to catch every word. At least I could share what I learned with Ryan. It would feel good to have something to tell him this evening at dinner. Was Kevin's eagerness to seize control motivated by more than just corporate maneuvering? More importantly, had it led him to kill his boss?

Finally, he hung up the phone and put it in his pocket, then kicked at a stone on the ground with a frown. Crossing his arms over his chest, he eventually traipsed back to the house, full of purpose. He hadn't seen Bertie and me at all. Or at least he hadn't cared to acknowledge us.

I couldn't wait to tell Ryan about the conversation. A conversation that made Kevin look very guilty.

"Well, that was interesting," Bertie said, leaning back on the bench of the picnic table and soaking up the heat. "Maybe we should move Kevin to the top of the list?"

"It seems like all of them have some motivation. I don't know which one had enough, though."

Bertie stood finally and stretched her back. "I better get back inside before I overheat. Think I'll go find Meg and see if she needs cheering. Other than getting her out of the house on Tuesday, let me know if there's anything else I can do to help with the party."

"Will do," I said as I followed her in. The heat was already getting to me, too. If I sat outside much longer, I'd cook my own goose. Bertie headed towards Meg's bedroom and I headed to the kitchen to do a little planning.

I grabbed a glass of iced tea out of the fridge and settled into a barstool with my notebook, determined to come up with a plan for our dinner with Ryan and Ty, along with a plan for Aunt Meg's birthday dinner. I knew all her friends would want to bring their own signature dishes, potluck style, but I wanted to do a few special things as well. At least one entrée and one dessert. There could never be too much food at a party, I reasoned.

But focusing on food proved difficult for once. My mind kept returning to the problem of Barry's murder, and how to get these people back to California...or jail... as quickly as possible. Based on the conversation I'd overheard between Tori and Barry, and the fact that they shared an intimate moment the night before his death, I had strong suspicions about Tori. It was hard to tell what her actual feelings about anything were, so I didn't feel very confident that I could figure out what was actually going on with her.

Questions also came up around Eric. He seemed obsessed with Tori but in a quiet, brooding way, and I could easily see that being a reason for him to want Barry out of the picture. He seemed nice enough, and I struggled to imagine him killing someone, but that didn't mean he didn't do it. And then there was Kevin. I was not fond of the man. Not one bit. He'd been rude since the beginning and he seemed completely unaffected by Barry's death, not to mention totally motivated to take over in Barry's absence. I didn't know if he'd been anywhere near Barry when he went over the rail, though, even though Tori had said he was. Just because Tori said it didn't make it true, however.

If only I could remember where everyone had been, if only I had been watching more closely when it happened.

I polished off my tea and still hadn't written down a single food idea, so I got up and finished cleaning the dishes from the day before, hoping it would help me think.

An hour later, after finishing with the mess from the dinner party, I was no closer either to knowing what to make for dinner or to who killed Barry. I sighed and wiped my hands on a dishrag. Grabbing my notebook, I went looking for Aunt Meg and Bertie to say goodbye.

What I needed to do was tool around the grocery store. Maybe the sight of all that food would give me some ideas.

Chapter Fifteen

Twenty minutes later, I was slowly pushing a cart around H.E.B. without a plan or a purpose, completely lost in my own thoughts. No matter how much I wanted to shake it, I kept thinking about Barry's death. Of all the bad luck, here I was once again wrapped up in murder. I hated the death and the sadness, but for whatever reason, my mind loved the puzzle part of it all.

If only I'd been paying more attention at the winery. Would I have been able to stop his death from happening? Would I have been able to see who pushed him? Or was he pushed at all? Maybe he was frightened, maybe he took a wrong step, or lost his balance. He had been drinking quite a bit of wine that day, so it was certainly possible that it was all just a gruesome accident.

But it didn't feel right.

There was too much animosity, too many people with motives to want him dead. No, I was certain that whenever Ryan finally found the answer to who killed Barry Golding, and I didn't doubt he would, that it would be someone from his group.

A butternut squash caught my eye as I was ambling through the produce section, and my cooking brain finally started kicking. I could do a simple roasted chicken with homemade butternut squash ravioli in sage brown butter. It sounded delicious. A little heavy perhaps, but decadent and classy. A dish that was comforting, something I knew all four of us could appreciate at present. I would cut the richness of the main dish with a simple kale salad with a tangy vinaigrette, and fruit for dessert. Watermelons were in season and I grabbed a big green one as I left the produce aisle.

The ravioli was a fussy choice, and a complicated one. But I needed more time to think, and I always did my best thinking in the kitchen. This afternoon I could continue to puzzle through the problems of who killed Barry and how to get more business while I sifted flour and rolled pasta dough.

A few minutes later, as I was searching for a good parmesan for the ravioli, a woman caught my eye. She stood next to a small stand and had samples to offer. She looked a little desperate, and I could understand why. The store was nearly empty at this time of day. As soon as she realized I was looking at her station, she beamed.

"Good afternoon," she said, her voice like velvet. "Would you like to try a sample?"

I abandoned my quest for the perfect cheese and angled my cart toward her. I was always in the mood for a sample. "Sure! What've you got?"

The woman launched into an enthusiastic description of her offering. "I have a delightful truffle infused honey. The honey is local lavender honey, and the truffle is sourced directly from France," she explained, as she took a small cracker, placed a thin slice of parmesan on it, and drizzled honey over the whole thing. Her eyes sparkled with the kind of passion only a true food lover possesses. It was a look I knew well. I took the piece she offered me, smelling it first and then gently putting it into my mouth with my eyes closed so I could concentrate my full attention on the flavors that danced on my tongue. The richness of the truffles and the smooth sweetness of the honey melded in an unexpected yet perfectly balanced way.

"This is amazing," I told her sincerely, already picturing how I could drizzle it over the roasted chicken to really elevate the dish. Not to mention using it in the salad dressing I would create, tying the entire meal together. I thanked her, quickly grabbing a jar of the honey and a chunk of aged Parmesan before heading off, excited that I'd found the perfect ingredient to pull the whole meal together.

As I made my way through the store, I continued to think about the sample. I never would have known that something as decadently delicious as truffle infused honey existed if I hadn't tried a sample in the store. But now that I knew about it, I would add it to my regular stock for catering. It was such a unique and intense flavor pairing, I could imagine using it for all kinds of dishes, sweet as well as savory. Thinking about all the possibilities as I meandered through the store, my brain started lighting up with ideas.

And then it hit me. The sample had gained the honey company a new customer! And what *I* needed were new customers! I realized that not enough people in Sugar Creek knew Deep in the Heart Catering existed. Sure, I had a website and did some advertising. But that was mostly for people looking for a local caterer specifically. I thought about all the people who turned to one of the local restaurants for catering because they didn't know another option existed. What I needed to do was give them a sample, let them see what else was on offer in town.

All the drama with the California group, the death, and Bertie's presence had distracted me mightily the last few days, but the truth was that I didn't have a single job on the books and I did not know where my next paycheck was going to come from. Samples could make the difference between success and failure of my business. I could feel it in my bones.

I absently pushed my cart through the aisles, missing things I needed because I was so lost in thought. What a great idea! Samples were always a great way to introduce a business, especially a food business. I knew that the bread and butter of many catering companies were steady corporate clients, but I hadn't gotten a single business account yet. I decided that tomorrow morning I would take around samples to a few local businesses and see if I could entice them to place an order. Even a couple of sandwich boxes or buffet style drop off jobs would bring in more cash. I would make up some gourmet sandwiches and salads, maybe cookies to sweeten the deal, and take them around.

Finally, I finished shopping. I'd come up with a good dinner plan and an excellent plan for finding new business, although all thoughts of Aunt Meg's birthday party had gone out the window. Oh well, I still had a couple of days to figure out the details for *that*. Checking the time, I hurried to get groceries into my car, suddenly aware that I was pressing my luck if I wanted to roast a whole chicken before the boys came over for dinner.

Twenty minutes later, I'd given Cocoa his tribute of puppy treats and pets for having held down the fort without us, put all the food away, and pulled my apron on.

I was ready to cook.

Using big kosher salt crystals, I salted the chicken all over and put it on a pan uncovered in the refrigerator. Ideally, I liked to do this the day before cooking it to really let the salt get in and tenderize the meat, but I didn't have the time, so I would have to make do. Next, I pulled out the heavy butternut squash and peeled and cubed it, then placed it all in a steamer basket over boiling water. The steaming water was hot on my face and after I put the lid on and set a timer, I wiped the sweat away and sat down for a minute to collect my thoughts.

And there were a lot of them swirling around. Dinner plans, sample ideas, and thoughts about murder all whipped into a frenzy. I took a long drink of water, trying to clear my head before getting back to work.

I was a person who delighted in order. It pained me to have so many things so totally out of control at once. But I knew that sometimes there was nothing to do but to push through the chaos, taking one small step at a time until things sorted themselves out. Right now, I was in the center of an enormous ball of wound up string, everything tangled and jumbled. It was uncomfortable, but if I just kept going one step at a time, I would get the pieces all back into order.

With that thought, I stood and went back to my kitchen work. The timer went off, and I pulled the squash out, letting it cool slightly before combining it with ricotta, a splash of cream, a sprinkle of Parmesan for that sharp cheesy edge, and a pinch of nutmeg to add depth. The mixture was a warm, inviting orange, and it smelled like autumn. I tasted it, adjusting the seasoning with a little more salt and a crack of black pepper.

Just as I put the chicken in the oven, I heard the front door open. Cassie walked in, her arms full of the day's mail and a tired but content smile on her face. "Smells like heaven in here," she commented, setting the mail on the counter and kicking off her shoes. "How was your day? Anything interesting happen after I left Primrose House?"

I told her about the overheard conversation between Kevin and someone on the phone and we both puzzled over it while I mixed flour and eggs together for the pasta, gradually adding a bit of olive oil and water to get the perfect dough consistency.

"I don't know. My money is still on the blonde," Cassie said. "It's too suspicious that she was standing right next to him, arguing with him. And like you said, her excuse of being confused and not remembering what happened seem out of character."

I nodded as I sealed the spaces on the pasta sheets between the filling with a small fork and cut the squares. "What I don't understand, though, is why she would kill someone who she was trying to run away with? I guess they could have broken up, or had some falling out that I'm not aware of. But it doesn't really add up in my mind."

"What we need to do is some poking around. It'd be so easy, what with them staying at your aunt's B&B and all."

I shook my head. "The problem is, they are *constantly* there. I haven't seen any of them leave the place other than for the dinner party since they arrived. I would've thought they'd want to do some sightseeing while they're here, but all they do is work and argue and drink. They could have done that back in California without dragging us into all their chaos."

"Well, maybe we should convince them to do something else. Get them out of there for the day, or even an hour, and get Maria or Bertie to do some snooping." She knew Aunt Meg well enough that she didn't even hint at *her* snooping on her guests.

It wasn't a terrible idea. I had to give her that much. But my mind was working too hard on other problems to brainstorm creative ways to get surly guests out of the B&B.

"If you can think of something, I'm all for it. But I'm pretty overloaded at the moment. I don't have the bandwidth to orchestrate that sort of thing."

Cassie got her thinking face on, and I started to worry. "Nothing crazy, Cass, alright? I can't handle crazy at present."

Her eyes danced. "Okay. Sure. I'll figure something out. But right now, it's only fifteen minutes to go-time! I hope you're at a stopping point, cause Ryan and Ty will be here any minute and you need to go clean yourself up, girl," Cassie said and pointed at me with a laugh.

I looked down and realized I was covered head to toe in flour and who knew what else. I laughed, checked the chicken, and laid out the things I would need for the last minute brown butter sauce, and then went to go clean myself up, giddy that Ryan would be with me momentarily.

CHAPTER SIXTEEN

When I came out of my room a while later, I found Cassie had set the mood for our evening with candles and a lovely vintage vase of fresh flowers on the coffee table. She wore a pretty red wrap dress and was opening a bottle of wine. She poured me a glass, and I took it from her. "Cheers," she said.

I smiled, and we clinked glasses. The doorbell rang as we took our first sip. Cassie smiled. "Right on time."

As she moved to the door to let Ryan and Ty in, I took the chicken out of the oven to rest and heated the pasta water to cook the ravioli. Ryan came into the kitchen, his big manly presence delicious in the tiny space. I leaned in for a kiss.

"How's my favorite chef?" he asked.

"Better, now that you're here."

Cassie got them each a drink, and I finished up the cooking, placing the ravioli in a pretty dish and slicing the chicken and arranging it on a platter. Cassie and I carried the dishes to the table, and we all sat down to eat.

Ryan, taking a generous bite of the chicken, let out a satisfied mmm. "I've never had truffle before. That's an incredible taste."

Cassie nodded as she slid a ravioli into her mouth and closed her eyes. "This is nuts, lady. I can't believe you wield this kind of culinary magic."

I laughed and blushed, took a bite of the tangy salad with hints of honey and truffle. I had to admit; it *was* pretty darn good.

Ty laughed as Cocoa made a hopeful round under the table, looking for any dropped morsels. "Even Cocoa approves of the dinner. Look at him go, the little scavenger."

I couldn't help but smile, basking in the moment's warmth. "Cooking for you guys, seeing you enjoy the food—it's the best part of my day. It makes all the craziness worth it."

As we continued to eat, Cassie turned the direction of our conversation toward what was surely on all our minds.

"Ty told me that the coroner finished with Mr. Golding," she said. "Did he have any helpful information?"

Ryan wiped his mouth and swallowed a sip of his wine, throwing a quick glance at Ty. Ty shrugged and gave Ryan a sideways smile. Ryan said, "they tested his blood alcohol level, and it was elevated, of course. But not enough to make us think he fell because he was drunk. I think you're right, Abby. I think someone loosened that rail intending to kill him. Or killing someone, at least. It's premature to assume that Barry was the intended victim, although from what I've seen of the rest of the group, I'd be surprised if it intended toward anyone else."

"I didn't notice anyone spending time over by the rail. Although I was pretty busy with cooking and everything," I told him.

Ryan nodded. "No one we talked to at the winery saw anything that looked like someone tampering with the rail. It might have happened before y'all got to Mark and Sheila's place too. The group has been in Sugar Creek since Thursday, right? So that leaves plenty of time for someone to sneak off down the road to do a little premeditated sabotage. I asked Mark and Sheila, but of course they noticed nothing. I'm sure they would've had that rail fixed immediately if they'd known."

It made sense, and it seemed like trying to figure out that part of the Barry's death was a wild goose chase.

"You said you overheard a conversation that might be important?" Ryan asked after he'd scraped his fork along his plate and licked it clean.

"Oh, ho! Seems to me like someone finally realized what an asset we are, Abby," Cassie said with a smug smile. "Maybe we aren't such bad sleuths after all."

She was pushing her luck, and I gave her a look before answering Ryan's question. "Kevin was talking on the phone today. I was nearby and heard him. He was talking about how now that Barry is out of the way, he wants to move forward with something that Barry didn't approve of. Sounds like he's trying to take over their company, take it public? I don't know if it's a reason for him to have killed his boss, though."

"Eric had something interesting to say along those lines," Ryan said as he leaned back in his chair. "He said that he'd found out Barry hadn't come by the technology that the company is built on honestly. I pried for more information but he claims not to know much, other than that Barry stole the technology from a company he used to work for called Innocore. He thought maybe Barry's death could have something to do with that."

We were all silent. The conversation from Kevin I'd heard earlier took on new meaning as I processed this information. It looked more and more like Kevin might have killed his boss to gain control of NexTech Dynamics, especially if he'd found out about Barry's past. But just because Eric knew, didn't mean that Kevin knew as well.

"Did Eric say how he found all this out? Do you think he could have anything to do with the other company? Did he work there or know someone who did? How did he know about Barry stealing the technology?" This was a lot of important stuff and I wanted every single detail. I loved that we were finally all working together rather than trying to hide our prying. It made things so much easier, and it made us a team. Judging by the ridiculous grin on Cassie's face, she felt the same way. She and Ty held hands tightly as they listened to Ryan.

Ryan laughed at my barrage of questions. "We're looking into *everyone* right now, trying to find connections. But I don't think Eric worked there. I think he just found out about Barry's past."

"The other interesting thing we found, that goes along with all this..." Ty started, and then eyed Ryan, unsure of whether he should continue.

Cassie and I looked from Ryan to Ty, watching something pass back and forth between them, something that, from the looks of it, had been a topic of conversation on more than one occasion between them.

Finally, Ryan sighed. "I don't think we could stop them if we tried," he said as he fiddled with his fork. "Besides, things have changed. That's pretty clear." Ryan met my eyes and gave me a warm smile. "You two have been a thorn in our sides these last months. You have been a handful and a half. But you've also been spot on sometimes, and you've been able to solve things we couldn't. Not to mention y'all look pretty doing it. Ty and I have been talking. He... and I... think it would be best if the four of us pooled our resources, worked more as a team, rather than working at cross purposes. So what I'm saying is, let's start over from here on out, ladies, alright? Let's think of ourselves as a team. You two are, from here on out, considered honorary members of the Sugar Creek police force."

Cassie just about jumped out of her seat. I squeezed Ryan's hand, my heart thumping wildly.

"Until you do something that makes me think otherwise," he warned. "And this does not give you any official powers whatsoever. We are not making this official in any way and no one else is to know about it. This is just an arrangement between the four of us and meant to stay that way. Alright, Ty, you can continue."

Cassie bit her lip and bounced in her chair. She shot me an excited look that I returned. Finally, some recognition of our sleuthing talents.

Ty finally continued. "We had a look through Mr. Golding's files and emails. Is seems he was going ahead with the sale of the company to a private firm without the knowledge of the rest of the group. From what Eric and Kevin said, they were in Sugar Creek to decide on whether to stay private or go public, but from the look of the emails and documents on Mr. Golding's laptop, he had already sold the company, or was in the final stages of it."

"That makes Kevin look even more suspicious," I mused. "Especially if Eric told him, or if he found out about what Barry was up to."

I stood and began clearing dishes, and the other three did the same. After I put everything away, I took out a bowl of juicy watermelon slices from the fridge and put it on the table between us. The fruit was deliciously cold and satisfying after our heavy meal.

"So, you had time to talk to that other couple from the B&B about last night? Did they have anything interesting to say?" I asked Ryan as we all dug in.

He nodded. "They said they left the winery before Barry died, that they only heard about it afterward from the other guests."

I stopped chewing and frowned, trying hard to remember the whole evening in detail. "That isn't true! I remember seeing them sitting there after I called you. After Barry had died."

"Are you sure?" Ty asked.

"Positive. Why would they lie about that, though?" I replied.

"Maybe they didn't want to get involved? I don't know, they seemed to keep to themselves quite a bit. Maybe they just didn't want to get sucked into the investigation. They might have been worried that y'all would make them stick around, too," Cassie said, her eyes growing wide. "You don't think they could have been involved, do you?"

I put down my watermelon, suddenly ill at the thought that they'd left town and might have been involved in Barry's death. For all I knew, they could be back in California already. I took a deep breath and calmed the fear. Shaking my head, I said, "I doubt it. They didn't even know each other, right? No, I think they just wanted to get away from the drama. I think that's why they checked out this morning."

"What? They checked out?" Ryan's eyebrows shot up and he looked nervous. "I thought they were booked through Tuesday."

"They were, but they checked out early today. Right after you talked to them, actually."

He placed a watermelon rind on the plate and stared into space, deep in thought. "I wonder now if I should have made them stay as well." He shrugged his shoulders. "Probably nothing else there, anyway. Still, I don't like that they left before we have this thing figured out."

As we all finished our watermelon in silence, Ty's phone buzzed. He frowned when he looked at it. "I'm so sorry, but it looks like they need me down at the station."

Ryan frowned. "Anything important?"

Ty laughed. "I doubt it. Mrs. Winters again. But I'm on call, so it's my turn." He stood and stooped to give Cassie a quick kiss. "Sorry I have to leave, babe. Thanks so much for dinner, Abby." He gave me a smile and bent to give Cocoa a few quick goodbye pets before grabbing his hat and heading out into the night.

Cassie, Ryan, and I chatted as we cleaned up the dinner dishes. I gave Cocoa a few scraps of chicken, which he was very grateful for. Between the leftovers and what Ty had given him, I hoped he wouldn't have a stomachache in the night. But I couldn't help but spoil the pup a little. Thoughts about how lonely and emaciated he'd been when he'd found me crept up from time to time and tugged on my sympathy. At least he was living a good life now.

"I'm going to take Cocoa for a walk," Cassie said after all the dinner mess was clean and headed to the closet to grab the leash. Immediately, Cocoa began dancing around her feet, letting out excited yips. "A nice *long* walk," she added with a grin.

I took the hint, and we settled in to smooch on the couch for a bit. Kissing Ryan was like nothing I'd ever experienced with another man. There was a delicious spark there, something deeper than our lips meeting. Sure, we'd had our differences around murder investigations, but beneath it all, we were very much the same. We cared about the truth, we cared about our town, and we cared about justice. It was a sturdy base for the budding relationship between us, giving it more solidity than the few passing relationships I'd had in the past.

After what was indeed a long while, Cassie finally came back with Cocoa, making copious amounts of noise as she came inside. I laughed at her as she tripped through the door. Cassie was nothing but trouble and I loved her to death.

"I better get going," Ryan said, rubbing my back lightly. "There's a lot of work to do around this murder still. I want to get back to the station and see if the background checks we requested have come in yet. The faster we can get this figured out, the faster we can get them on their way."

I nodded and leaned into his shoulder. He wrapped his arms around me, kissing the top of my head. I could have stayed in his arms all night. But solving the murder was the most important thing. I pulled away after a moment and kissed his cheek.

"Good luck, Sheriff."

He grabbed me and pulled me in for one last long kiss. "Sweet dreams, honey."

Chapter Seventeen

By Monday morning, I'd almost forgotten Cassie's idea about getting the California group out of the B&B so Bertie and Maria could snoop, until I emerged from my room with sleep still blurring my mind. I would bet my best knife she'd been up waiting for me for a while by the caffeine-induced gleam in her eye.

"I figured it out!" she cried from where she hovered by the coffeemaker. "You and I are going to set up a sightseeing tour. I'll get Ed Morton to give us a lift over to Fredericksburg or something. We can take them to the wildflower center or a beer garden. Something real touristy. He owes me a favor."

I arched an eyebrow, wondering just how many people owed Cassie a favor in this small town.

Cocoa bounced around at our feet, clearly as excited as Cassie was about her new idea. Too bad he didn't realize he wasn't going to be included in this adventure.

"I don't know Cass, I've got a lot to do today. I was going to make samples..."

"Come on Abby, this is important! I already talked to Kate and she can watch the store for me this morning. It'll be perfect. Bertie and Maria can search the rooms while we're gone." She got a sly look on her face. "And it'll give Aunt Meg a little time to herself, too. I know that's important for her right now."

She had me there. "Fine, but I only want it to take the morning. I need to get samples done. I'm all out of customers and it's only a matter of time before I'm out of money, too."

She did a happy dance and then gave me a hug. "Don't worry Abbs. You're bound to get a job anytime now. I can feel it in my bones."

She shook her body as if a shiver was running up her spine and I laughed, but felt a little shiver of my own. I moved to the coffeepot and poured myself a cup of coffee, drinking deeply, knowing I would need plenty of fuel to keep up with Cassie and her plans.

Poor Cocoa. If only he knew he was going to be left behind. But then my face brightened as I realized the entire group of B&B guests would be gone with us for the day, so Cocoa should be able to hang out with Aunt Meg and Bertie without anyone complaining. And if he wasn't wanted, I could always zip him back home after he'd said hello.

The three of us headed to Cassie's truck after getting ready for the day. I drove and Cassie made phone calls as we made our way through the nearly empty early morning streets of Sugar Creek. By the time we arrived at the B&B, we had it all planned out. Ed, who owned the Two-Step Through Texas tour company and who'd gone to school with Cassie and I, would pick us up in his mini tour bus in an hour and take us over to Fredericksburg until after lunch. We were lucky we'd chosen to ask on a Monday morning, seeing as it was still tourist season. I'm sure he would have been booked solid otherwise.

Unfortunately for us, the California group had no interest in playing along with our plans.

When we walked into Primrose House a little while later with Cocoa tucked between the two of us, we found the group angrily arguing in the front room. Maria was there too, dusting in the corner without them noticing. Her face lit up when Cassie and I walked in. We quickly whispered our plan to her, which she enthusiastically agreed with. She took Cocoa with her down the hall to find Aunt Meg and Bertie and Cassie and I steeled our nerves and she interrupted the din of chaos with a loud whistle. I flinched, but was grateful for her bravery. *I* never could have interrupted them.

"Alright, folks. This morning, my friend Abby and I are going to be providing an exclusive tour of the hill country, free of charge!"

Aunt Meg had come up behind us. She tugged on my arm and I turned to her. "What are you doing, Abby?"

I leaned over and said quietly, "We're giving you a break. One you desperately need. You and Bertie and Maria can take your time, clean up around here, have a little girl-time. Maybe do a little snooping." I laughed when her eyebrows shot up. "Just kidding!"

Bertie and Maria knew I wasn't kidding, though. They'd gotten their instructions, and they were ready to investigate. I could tell by the way Bertie waggled her eyebrows at me with a gleam in her eyes.

The group all whined and complained. "I'm sorry, but we're in the middle of something important here," Tori replied and turned away from us.

I glanced over at Eric. I could see his laptop pulled up to a YouTube video of men playing video games and yelling at each other. Yep, lots of important things going on *there*.

I sighed and put my hands on my hips. I'd known this wouldn't be easy. "Okay, well, this is the day that the... repairs are done on Primrose House and we can't have y'all here right now." A lightbulb went on. "How about a trip to the coworking space in Johnson City?"

"Do they have standing desks?" Tori screeched and immediately started packing her things into her bag.

"I don't know, but we will find out." Maybe this would be easy after all. I threw a sly smile over to Cassie and she grinned and gave me a thumbs-up.

Ed showed up just as a group finished packing their bags and tumbled out onto the porch.

"Alright, folks, y'all ready for some amazing sightseeing?" he said with a big warm Texas smile.

"No, we're not doing that anymore," Cassie said. "Do you mind taking us over to the business center in Johnson City? You know that coworker place? With the coffee and the Pilates?"

His smile waned, and he was clearly thrown for a loop at the change in plans, but as he opened the door of his small luxury bus he shrugged. "Whatever you say, Miss Divine. Your wish is my command."

She gave him a sweet smile and a pat on the arm before she climbed into the bus and the rest of us followed.

Once again, the group was silent on the way to Johnson City. It wasn't a long drive, but long enough that they should've been sharing some sort of social moment. Instead, Eric and Tori were both on their phones, Cheryl looked absently out the window, and Kevin nervously drummed his hands on his bag, so long and so loud that I was tempted to rip it away from him.

Never let them see you sweat. I wasn't about to let these people know they ruffled my feathers. I just hoped that Bertie and Maria were making progress on finding clues and that this wasn't all a waste of time. It grated on me when I thought about what else I could be doing with my morning.

I felt bad for the people at The Synergy Station as I watched the crew from NexTech Dynamics get out of the bus when we finally arrived. They were sullen, the lot of them. I just hoped they didn't get into any fistfights while we were here. It would be so embarrassing.

Cassie set about checking them in for the morning of work and I overheard Tori mumbling about why couldn't they have been there from the beginning. This was a much better place than the stuffy B&B. I agreed. It would've been much better having them over here rather than bothering us at Primrose House.

While I waited for Cassie to fill out paperwork, I scanned the area and saw that they had a kitchen space and several dining tables near the front where the people who worked in the space could eat and relax. And then a lightbulb went off. *The people who worked in the space.* I would bet at least some of these people needed catering occasionally. Lucky for me, I had some business cards and a few flyers with me.

Once Cassie finished checking the group in, I moved to the counter to talk to the receptionist.

"Hi, my name is Abby Hirsch, and I have a catering company over in Sugar Creek. I'm looking for some new business clients and I was wondering if it would be okay with you if I left some of my flyers and cards here, in case any of your patrons need catering."

Her eyes brightened. "Oh, that would be great. Actually, we host the Chamber of Commerce here once a month, and usually bring in something from a restaurant, but if you're competitive with their prices, I bet my manager would love to have you cater instead. Leave me one of your cards and brochures too, and I'll have her call you."

I was thrilled. The day wasn't a total waste after all.

Cassie and I hunkered down on a couch near the front door and waited. "How long are we supposed to do this?" I asked her, "and why do we need to be here too? Couldn't we have just dropped them off?"

Cassie twirled the strap of her purse around and around. "Probably, but I felt like it would be best if we kept an eye on them since they're all under investigation... and we *did* take them out of Sugar Creek and all. Strictly speaking, I think that was illegal."

My face blushed, and I mentally slapped my forehead. Why hadn't I thought about that? Ryan would be so mad if he knew what we'd done. Yep, that was probably illegal. "Good thinking."

We hung out together, talking quietly. After a while I was so bored that I could've chewed my own arm off, so when my phone rang I jumped to answer it, hoping it would be something, anything, interesting. I stood and paced as I accepted the call, hoping against hope it wasn't a telemarketer.

"Deep in the Heart Catering," I answered in my most upbeat voice.

"Hi, I'm calling because I have a situation and I really need a party catered, but it's a rush kind of thing. It's for tomorrow at lunch, for a party of sixty people. It's for the Blanco Audubon Society annual gathering. We had a caterer, but they canceled on us at the last minute and I'm at my wit's end! It's for a charity luncheon that we charged a hundred dollars a plate for, so barbecue and Mexican just won't cut it. Please, please, say you'll take it! You're my only hope."

Just call me Obi-Wan Kenobi.

The woman ran out of breath or she probably would've continued to talk. My stomach twisted. It was a huge job. It would be huge money, much needed money. And no doubt a huge headache for a party so large. And for tomorrow at lunch, no less. I chewed my lip.

"Well, ma'am, there's no way I can do a plated meal for that large a crowd on such a short notice. But I could do a buffet style service. What kind of food were you planning to serve?" I crossed my fingers and my eyes and everything else I could think of that I could indeed do a buffet service with less than twenty-four hour's notice. I might have to call in some troops. I bet Bertie would love to help if no one else was available.

"Something simple, but classy. The caterer who just quit was going to serve chicken piccata and some other things. I think pasta and a veggie side. And lava cakes." She moaned as she said it. "Oh, they're gonna be so disappointed. I told everybody about the lava cakes. I don't suppose you could do lava cakes?"

I was silent. Sixty lava cakes would be a stretch on a good day with a commercial kitchen. "Where is this event being held?"

"It's at the Blanco Convention Hall. We have use of their kitchen from ten until two if you need it."

That changed everything. I smiled. "I might be able to work something out." Kitchen space would make a big difference. I wouldn't have to worry about how to keep things hot and cold leading up to the event, one of my biggest headaches as a caterer. It would free me up quite a bit.

"I'd be happy to pay you extra," she added when I didn't continue right away.

A lightbulb went on. "Yes, I charge a ten percent rush fee for anything under twenty-four hours. If that's alright with you." I kicked myself for throwing that last bit in. What I wanted was to appear confident, but it was still hard for me. Maybe I'd get to that level of confidence someday. A girl can dream.

"That's no problem. The important thing is that we get *something* here. *I* certainly can't feed everyone," she said with a high-pitched trill of laughter. After I agreed, she gave me the details of the event, and I hung up the phone, elated.

Finally, I had another job.

Chapter Eighteen

If it grated on me to be stuck with the California people before, it downright ate me alive now that I had an enormous job sitting on my shoulders. I pulled out my notebook and started making plans. At least I could do *something* while we waited.

I would go ahead with chicken piccata, since that's what they were expecting. It would be easy enough in buffet form. I could serve it with a Greek orzo pasta salad and roasted vegetables. Briefly, I wondered if it was a good idea to serve a poultry course to the Audubon people, but since that's what they'd had planned before, I decided not to worry about it. I'd definitely do a good vegetarian option too, though, just in case. Leaning into the Greek pasta idea, maybe a baked feta with Greek seasonings and roasted tomatoes? It all depended on what I could easily get from the grocery store. There was no time to order anything or go into a bigger city to shop.

I thought I could probably do the lava cakes if I could get my hands on some commercial muffin tins. Aunt Meg probably didn't have enough for sixty, but I would check. If that didn't work, I could ask Ellie if I might borrow some for the day. It'd be easier than trying to buy them this close to the event.

Planning consumed me until, suddenly, Cassie smacked my leg. "Time to go," she said, pointing outside to where Ed had pulled up next to the curb.

"Thank goodness. I've got a million things I need to do." I'd told Cassie about the last minute job and I knew she was feeling the pressure for me. She hustled the group of B&B guests quickly outside and I was amazed at her techie-wrangler skills.

As we were stepping onto the bus, I heard Tori whispering to Cheryl in front of me. Cheryl's face was ghostly pale, and I wondered what they were talking about, but not wanting to appear too nosy, I refrained from leaning over to hear better. It would be way too obvious. But as we walked onto the bus and just before I sat down beside Cassie, I caught a couple of phrases.

"I know about your brother," Tori hissed.

"You know nothing, Tori. Shut up." Her face was blank, but a fury danced in her eyes, a fury that I wouldn't want to be on the other side of.

Cheryl had been following Tori to the back of the bus, but abruptly veered back and sat in the seat across from me. She closed her eyes and hugged her bag to her chest as the bus doors shut and we started off.

"Are you okay?" I asked her a few minutes later when I realized her eyes were still closed. Her color didn't look good.

"Fine. Just a little homesick, I guess." She opened her eyes and looked out the window. "This entire trip was a huge mistake."

"I'm sorry to hear you think that. Texas can be a lovely place if you open yourself up to it."

"Oh, it's not the place that's the problem. It's the company," she said as she threw a glance back toward her coworkers, who were all three once again wrapped up in their devices.

"Tori said something about your brother?" I asked her. I

remembered her talking about some family trouble back on the night of Barry's murder.

Cheryl's eyes glazed over and I immediately regretted asking. Why couldn't I keep my questions to myself? She bit her lip, searching for what to say, not meeting my gaze. "Oh, my brother is...sick. And Tori found out. It's kind of a family secret. I don't really want to talk about it, if it's all the same to you."

"Of course, I'm sorry. If you need to talk, or need anything else, just let me know."

Cheryl turned to me, her eyes full of tears. "Thank you. You all sure have been sweet. It's a pleasant change from..." She glanced back at her coworkers again. "Sorry we had to come here and ruin things for you."

I shrugged it off and let her be alone with her thoughts, partly because I could tell she needed some peace, but also partly because I needed to focus all of my attention on the monster catering job that lay before me. The next twenty-four hours were going to be grueling, a serious test of my skills.

I only hoped I could pull it all off.

As soon as we got back to Primrose House, I would need to take stock of all the staples I had, make a list of what I needed, and head to the store. There was no time to dilly-dally. I would also need to borrow the Connolys' van once again. There was no way I could transport everything I needed for a party of sixty in my tiny Honda. This part of my business was getting really old. Every time I called them up to borrow their vehicle, I felt guiltier than the time before.

I pulled out my phone to make the call and Sheila answered right away.

"Hey, Abby! What a coincidence! I was just thinking about you!"

"Oh, really? What about?"

"Well, a couple of things. First, I wanted to check and see how y'all are doing with the death and that group of guests."

I blew out a breath and glanced behind me to the still silent and sullen group. "We're managing, but it's no picnic."

"Well, I'm sorry to hear that...I also wanted to talk to you because I'd like you to stop by the day after tomorrow so we can plan a wine tasting with fondue."

Smiling, I leaned back in my seat. My thoughts immediately kicked into high gear with ideas for new fondue possibilities. As crazy as the night of the party had been, I'd barely had time to process the catering aspect, but I'd loved doing the fondue dinner. "Sure, I'd love that. I should have time on Wednesday."

Then I frowned, remembering why I called. "I'm really sorry I have to ask to borrow the van again, and I swear I'm gonna get myself a proper vehicle soon, but would you mind if I borrowed the van again tomorrow until about two? I just got a big catering job and I don't think I can swing it otherwise."

Sheila paused. "Oh, Abby. I hate to say no to you, you know that, right? But we planned to go over to Austin to pick up some new supplies for the winery this afternoon and we'll be gone overnight. Probably won't be back until tomorrow evening."

Shoot. "That's okay, I understand. It really is time for me to look around for a vehicle," I said with a laugh. "Don't worry about it. I'll make it work with what I've got."

"I really am sorry. If we were going to be here, I'd say yes," she told me.

"I know it. Hey, it's fine. Okay, I better get going, but I'm looking forward to seeing you on Wednesday!"

"Sounds good. Say hi to your aunt for me!"

I hung up with Sheila and bit my lip, glancing out the window at the brown fields passing by. I couldn't wait for fall to arrive. The heat was really getting to me. Or maybe it was just pressure and frustration from my business and everything else that was happening.

"What happened? You look like you were sent for and couldn't go," Cassie said when she caught my sour look.

I sighed. "Sheila and Mark are using their van tomorrow." I perked up. "Hey, would you mind if I used your truck?"

Her face turned down. "I'm so sorry, lady, but I've got a special pre-look at an upcoming estate sale over in Kerrville tomorrow. I can't miss it."

I sighed. The only thing to do was to make it work with my coupe. I couldn't afford to rent something. Boy, I sure could make things tough for myself. Why hadn't I taken the time to get a catering vehicle already? I could've kicked myself.

We stopped by a sandwich shop to pick up lunch for everyone, so Aunt Meg wouldn't have to deal with it. When we got back to Primrose House, Cassie left to go back to her store, and I high-tailed it to the kitchen to once again take stock of everything we had as the others headed off to do whatever it was they did. I found Aunt Meg, Bertie, and Cocoa enjoying lunch in the kitchen and I told them about my job as I rushed around and made a list. My intensity must have scared them off because after they finished their salads, they skedaddled with Cocoa.

I barely noticed their absence, my mind was churning so wildly. I'd never contemplated charging a rush fee before, and it made me feel guilty. But I'd also never catered an event in less than twenty-four hours. Already my heart rate was skyrocketing just thinking about the work I was about to do. A buffet for sixty people, including lava cakes to finish the deal, all by noon the following day. It sounded overwhelming, but if I planned just right, it should end up being very lucrative, especially with the extra rush charge. I tried to focus on that.

I was just about to head to the store when Bertie came back in. "I wanted you to know that Maria and I were quite busy while you were gone. We were...cleaning...the guest rooms." She glanced around the room and lowered her voice, even though no one else was around. "We found some very interesting things."

I stopped writing, my eyes wide. With all the craziness of the new job, I'd completely forgotten why we'd been to Johnson City at all.

She slid onto a bar stool next to me. "Eric had some paperwork about another company with a lot of notes. It looked like he'd dug up something about Barry. We were thinking maybe he confronted Barry with it, or they had a fight about it at the winery? That maybe the whole thing was an accident?"

I nodded. "Ryan and Ty told us last night that Eric had found evidence that Barry had not come by the technology the company was built on legally. He thought it might be why Barry was trying to push a private deal without the consent of the others."

She leaned back and thought. "We're assuming that a person who worked with Barry was the one to kill him. But what if that isn't the case? What if it was somebody outside of the group entirely? Like someone who had to do with this other company, or the private sale?"

"I doubt it. The entire group has been here at the B&B almost exclusively. How would anyone even know they were here? Or that they would be at the winery that day? The loosened rail was almost certainly premeditated. And only his coworkers...and us...knew about the plans for the dinner party there. At least as far as I know."

Her face sagged, but then her eyes lit up. "We also found a sketchpad in Kevin's room. It was covered in doodles. But one doodle was done over and over. It was the words 'Innocore'. Which is the same name we found in Eric's notes."

My eyes shot up. "So Kevin *did* know about Barry's former company." I leaned against the counter to think. It could be the key to everything. I'd assumed before that Kevin hadn't known about Barry. But now I wondered when he'd found out about Barry's past. Was it before or after the man was murdered?

"I wonder if we could find anything out about this company, Innocore Solutions."

Bertie got a gleam in her eye. "They didn't dub me master

researcher at Bayberry Elementary for nothing! You have a few minutes to poke around at the googles with me?"

Regretfully, I shook my head. "Sorry, no can do. I really have to concentrate on the catering right now. I have way too much to do, and way too little time. But let me know what you find out! And if you want to get a taste of the catering business later, I'd be happy for some help. Totally up to you, though. No pressure. I want you to enjoy your vacation!"

Amusement danced in her eyes, and she smiled. "I'd love that! And trust me, this is the best vacation I've had in years! So much excitement!"

She left to go put her master researcher hat on and I finalized my shopping list and then hopped up to get on with my tasks. It was going to be a long day.

Chapter Nineteen

Shopping was getting very old, but at least today I was clearheaded and on a mission. I wanted to get in and out quickly and get back to the B&B to prep as much as I could before the end of the day. Once again, the place was nearly empty, and I flew through with my cart screeching, checking things off my list in a frenzy as I went. I felt a little like one of those contestants on a game show, but I was on the clock. When I pulled up to check out the clerk, who recognized me by this point, eyed my cart in horror as I began piling my goods onto her checkout stand.

"Y'all must be having some sort of party!"

I'd had the conversation with her before, but clearly she didn't remember. "I'm a caterer. This is for an event I'm catering."

Her eyes went wide as she continued to scan my purchases. "Some fancy things y'all got here. Woo wee."

Normally I loved small talk, but I was all out by this point, so I paid quickly with my business credit card and bagged my own groceries so I wouldn't have to sit and gab with the woman the rest of the day.

When I got back to the B&B, I immediately put everything

away and piled my cutting board high with vegetables that needed chopping. The feta and tomato dish and the chicken would have to be baked on-site tomorrow morning and the lava cakes would go into the oven over there once everyone had started on the lunch so they'd be nice and warm and gooey when served, but I could do a lot of the prep work now to make things easy on myself tomorrow. Every vegetable could be chopped, every piece of chicken could be pounded, the breading for the chicken could be mixed, and sauces could be made, and that is what I set about doing.

With all the hubbub around the catering job, I hadn't given a second's thought to Aunt Meg's party, and I burned with shame. At least I'd already invited everyone I wanted to, so I hadn't fallen down too terribly. I would still need to cook something and find some decorations for the place. Maybe I could pass that task off to Cassie or Maria.

But all of my plans came to a screeching halt a few minutes later when Maria came into the kitchen, her eyes full of tears.

"Oh, no, what's wrong?" I asked her.

"It's... the blonde woman. I went into her room to tidy for the evening. I knocked first and there was no answer, so I thought it was okay. But it is not okay. Not at all. The blonde woman is dead."

I nearly dropped my knife, and my free hand shot fast to my mouth. "Tori?"

She nodded, and tears started to fall.

"Does anybody else know?" I asked as I pulled out my phone to once again call Ryan.

"I don't think so. The rest of them are all working in the dining room."

I dialed as I followed Maria up the creaking stairs. I tried to be as quiet as possible. The last thing I wanted was for the rest of the group to get nosy and come upstairs with us. "Hey, Ryan," I said when he picked up. "Uh, I hate to say this, but..." I paused as I came to a stop at the door to Tori's room. Maria unlocked it and swung the door wide and I saw Tori lying facedown on the carpet, her arm out like she was reaching for something, and her face turned toward us. It was lifeless, puffy, and twisted in gruesome pain. "I think we have another murder victim."

"I'm on my way right now."

When I hung up the phone, Maria and I stared at each other a moment, tears in both of our eyes, and we moved to each other and hugged. It was an awful, awful thing to happen. Pulling away, I cautiously stepped inside the room. I probably shouldn't have even gone in, but I wanted to see if there was anything that could help me understand what had happened. I moved around the bed, careful not to touch anything, to get a better look. Her outstretched arm was reaching toward her purse, the contents of which were scattered all over the floor. I scanned the rest of the room but saw little else out of order.

"Okay, let's lock it back up until Ryan arrives," I told Maria. We headed back downstairs to wait for Ryan.

In the time we were upstairs, everyone in the house had moved to the front room. Eric and Kevin were sitting on the couch with their laptops out and Cheryl sat in a chair next to them, taking notes on her own laptop as the three of them talked. Aunt Meg and Bertie were in the far corner whispering and laughing.

"Uh oh," Aunt Meg said as looked at Maria and my faces. "What's going on now?"

Maria and I glanced at each other. It didn't matter if they knew now. Her door was locked and Ryan was on his way. "Tori is dead."

Eric shot up from the couch, his laptop sliding to the ground. "No!" he cried and raced up the stairs. Kevin's eyes grew wide and Cheryl's eyes immediately filled with tears.

"What in the world?" she said. "What is going on around here?" She stood and paced the room, suddenly growing wild. Her face turned angry, and she pulled at her hair.

"It seems that someone in your group is killing their coworkers off," I said as I glanced out the window, praying that Ryan would arrive fast. Things could get very heated very quickly with these people and I worried about our safety, especially since now we knew with certainty that one of the three of them was a killer.

Cheryl stopped pacing and whirled to glare and Maria and I. "Maybe it was one of you! For all *we* know, one of you could be some psycho serial killer who likes to kill guests. Anybody else end up dead around here lately?" she screeched.

Aunt Meg, Maria, and my eyes all grew wide.

"What? Are you kidding me? There were other deaths here? Does the sheriff know about this? I think we need to call the sheriff right now! This B&B is a death house!" Cheryl cried.

"Trust us, he knows. And what happened in the past had nothing to do with what's happening now. The sheriff is already on his way. You can talk to him when he arrives if you have questions about the B&B."

Lucky for us, Ryan pulled up just then, followed by yet another ambulance. I opened the door, and the EMTs rushed inside. Maria led the way up to Tori's room, and everyone else followed them.

The hallway was very crowded. Ryan stopped in the doorway and Tori's coworkers craned their necks around his body to see what was going on. I caught a glimpse of the EMTs bending over Tori's lifeless form on the floor. I prayed that I'd been wrong about her being dead. Maybe there was something they could do. But I highly doubted it. She'd seemed very dead a few moments before.

"Okay, folks, we're gonna need y'all to go back downstairs and wait," Ryan said as a third EMT squeezed around everyone and headed into the room. Grudgingly, Tori's coworkers headed back to the front room. Maria, Aunt Meg, Bertie, and I all followed. Nobody sat down. Kevin and Eric both paced. Cheryl stood by the window and looked out in a daze into the yard.

Our crew huddled in the corner and whispered. "What do you think happened?" Aunt Meg asked me.

Shrugging, I said, "I don't know for sure. I didn't see any blood, no obvious sign of foul play."

"But you're sure it was a murder? Not some sort of accident?"

Glancing around the room, I nodded. "I don't know why, exactly. Maybe because of Barry. But it feels very much on purpose to me. Did any of you see anything while I was gone? Was Tori around at all, or was she in her room the whole time?"

We'd only arrived back from the coworking space a little over an hour before, so there wasn't much time for whatever to have happened to happen. At least we knew that one of the three of them was responsible for Tori's death, assuming that she had indeed been murdered. And that also meant that one of the three of them was responsible for Barry, too.

"While you were at the store, she came down and made herself a smoothie."

Here was something. Could someone have poisoned her? My eyes shot again to the group of coworkers. The much *smaller* group of coworkers.

"Let's go into the kitchen." I hated to leave them alone, but I wanted to talk somewhere more private and have a look around.

We all headed down the hall. Aunt Meg moved to the coffeemaker and started making us coffee. As soon as I saw her measuring out the grounds, I craved it. Hot, tasty, fuel was exactly what I needed at present. I scanned the kitchen where I'd abandoned my catering prep work to follow Maria up to Tori's room a little while ago and my blood pressure shot up. But the catering would just have to wait.

"Tell me what you saw," I asked Maria as I moved around to the counter to put away the onion I'd been chopping.

"She came down only a few minutes after you left. I'd shown her how to use the smoothie machine, so she's been doing it herself the last few days. She made herself a smoothie, did not clean up after herself, and went right back upstairs with the drink."

I frowned and glanced around the kitchen. "And you cleaned up after her?"

"Yes. I'm sorry," Maria replied.

I gave her a warm smile. "There's nothing to apologize for! You were just doing your job. There was no way to know…" I trailed off as I caught sight of the bag of acai powder sitting near the blender.

"Do you remember what she used in her smoothie?" I didn't know yet how she'd died. But it seemed suspicious that she was dead so soon after eating something. Or drinking it? Do you eat a smoothie or drink it? Who knew?

"She used that powder we bought her," she said, pointing to the acai, "and some coconut water, and blueberries, I believe. I did not pay close attention."

I picked up the bag of acai powder and peered inside. I could see some tiny white flecks that I didn't think should be there. "Tori was the only person who used this acai all week, right?"

"As far as I know."

"That's convenient." I remembered the list of demands… requests…the group had given us when they'd arrived. The first line was about a severe peanut allergy. I wondered, was it Tori who was allergic to peanuts? Sealing up the bag, I put it on the counter in plain view. I didn't want to lose sight of it for even a second before I could tell Ryan about it.

"Thank you, Maria. Don't worry, this will all get figured out."

She nodded and wrapped her arms around herself.

"You think her smoothie poisoned her?" Bertie asked, sitting down on a bar stool with a cup of coffee that Aunt Meg handed her.

"Seems likely," I replied, taking a cup as well. I inhaled deeply and felt the fragrant steam loosening up my muscles. Taking a sip, I closed my eyes. My nerves were shot, my feet and back hurt, and it wasn't even close to five. This day just got crazier and crazier.

"It's absolutely bonkers to think that one of the three people in the other room is a killer," Bertie said as she sipped. Her eyes were glazed, her face more serious than I'd ever seen it.

We were all silent after that, trying to process the insanity that we were living. I felt bad for Bertie and wished now that I hadn't invited her for Aunt Meg's birthday after all.

Aunt Meg's birthday that was tomorrow...

Aunt Meg sat heavily on the kitchen chair, her eyes red rimmed with sadness and unshed tears. My heart ached for her. She just couldn't get a break. The last week had been a real struggle for her, but I knew that this was something all together different.

"Nobody has died in this house. Not since your Uncle Nolan."

"Tricia McBride died at the house."

"No, her body was *left* here. She didn't die here. And it was outside. I don't know why it's so different, but it is."

I nodded. I knew what she meant.

No matter what way you looked at it, we had another death on our hands. It was enough to make even the most cheerful person depressed.

CHAPTER TWENTY

After we'd all finished our coffee and I'd poured myself a second cup, Ryan finally came into the kitchen.

"We're done upstairs for now, although I'd like to treat Ms. Dennison's room as a crime scene for the time being, until we've had a chance to really go over everything. So if y'all would stay out and keep everyone else out, that would be much appreciated."

"So someone *did* murder her, then."

Ryan crossed his arms over his chest and frowned. "Technically, she died of anaphylactic shock. But I'd bet money it was more than an accident. For now, until we know more, I'd like to treat this as a murder investigation. Especially given what happened with Mr. Golding so recently."

I nodded and knew my instincts about the smoothie were probably right.

"I think you should see something," I told him. Picking up the bag of acai powder, I held it open for him to peer inside, explaining about the peanut allergy as I did. "I'm not sure she was the one who was allergic, or if that's even peanut in there. But it could be how she died."

He stared down into the bag with a frown. "So you think something in that bag poisoned her?"

I nodded.

"And you picked the bag up with your bare hands."

I nodded, much less enthusiastically this time, realizing my mistake. Ryan sighed. Being an honorary member of the police force wasn't really working out the way I'd thought it would.

Maybe I should turn in my badge. *Oh, yeah.* I didn't have one.

Ryan pulled a large ziplock out of the back of his pocket and held it open for me, and my cheeks blazed. Dropping the acai powder in, I tried to console myself with the thought that almost everyone in our group probably touched that bag over the last few days, between making Tori smoothies and cleaning up her messes when she made her own. It was likely that fingerprints wouldn't be too important one way or the other.

He sealed the bag up and labeled it with a sharpie that he pulled out of the other back pocket. Before we got any further in our conversation, we heard a ruckus from the front room. We all hurried down the hall to see what was happening, and found Eric and Kevin standing close, their bodies stiff and angry, like two bulls about to go at it.

"Why did you even like her, man? She was never going to go for you. Tori was way out of your league. Not to mention she was a cold hard…"

Eric lunged for Kevin with an angry growl before he could say another thing. I flinched as his shoulder connected to the older man's chest and they both crashed to the ground. The two of them wrestled around on the floor, both of them managing to land hard thudding blows on each other before Ryan stepped in to pull them apart.

The men both sat on the floor, glaring at each other. Eric's mouth was bleeding and Kevin's glasses were broken and lopsided on his face. He rubbed the back of his head.

Ryan put his hands on his hips and glared at them. "If you two can't find a way to keep your hands to yourselves while at this establishment, I'm going to have to take you down to the station."

"Why'd you do it, Kevin?" Eric cried, panting hard and dabbing at the blood seeping out of his lip. "Why'd you kill her? Did she know something about you? Did she find out you killed Barry? She didn't deserve it!" The last bit was laced with all the pain in the world. He nearly shouted it. And then he stood and flew up the stairs to his room.

Cheryl stood by the window, her face grim, her eyes darting back and forth to the room and the outdoors. I could tell all she wanted was to get the heck out of Sugar Creek and back to her home. I felt sorry for her.

"We are going to have to treat Primrose House as a crime scene for the time being," Ryan told Aunt Meg. "I'm sorry, but you can't have anyone else stay until we've finished our investigation. And it goes without saying," his eyes moved to Cheryl and Kevin. "But no one can leave town. I'd even say I'd like everyone to stay here at Primrose House as much as possible. No outings."

My heart sank. "We were planning on having a party here for Aunt Meg tomorrow night. Can we still do that?"

"Under the circumstances, I think it's best if y'all held off on your aunt's party for now. I'm so sorry, Abby. Now, if you folks don't mind talking with me a few minutes," he said to Cheryl and Kevin, "I'd like to speak with you about Ms. Dennison."

Kevin stood and dusted himself. With an angry glare, he grabbed his laptop and headed down the hall to the dining room. Ryan shot Cheryl a look and then followed Kevin down the hall.

At least I hadn't done any serious planning for the birthday party yet. I'd have to call up the friends I'd invited and reschedule, see if Cassie could get the band for another night. But I hadn't bought the food yet, so that was a bonus.

The EMTs came and went out the front door while the rest of us watched. Eventually, they brought Tori's body down on a stretcher covered in a sheet. Cheryl turned away. So did Aunt Meg.

I knew she was struggling mightily with this. She'd already been through a lot and the fresh death, in her own home, was pushing her to the brink, I could tell.

Ty set about searching everyone's rooms with another deputy. It could easily take them the rest of the day. Looking at the time, my heart did a little flurry. I needed to get back to work ASAP if I had any hope of making this lunch gig happen. I stood and stretched and started to head into the kitchen, but Bertie reached out a hand and stopped me.

"Do you have a minute to look at something?"

"Sure," I told her, following her to the computer in the corner of the room. She pulled the screen up to an old article in Forbes magazine. Between the blocks of text was a photo of a group of people all gathered for a picture outside a squat office complex. At the bottom was a sign that said "Innocore."

"That looks like Barry Golding, don't you think?" she said, pointing to the picture.

I squinted as I bent down to get a closer look. There had to be fifty people in the picture and it was hard to make faces out, but sure enough, a younger version of Barry Golding stood front and center in the group, his arm around the man next to him.

I nodded.

"And that one there? Doesn't he look familiar? He almost looks like the man who was here with his wife over the weekend. If you get rid of the glasses, let the hair grow out, no?" She pointed to someone else in the second row.

"Let me see." There was some resemblance, but the picture was old and grainy. It was hard to tell for sure. It was a stretch, and a big one, but probably worth looking into. Even if the man she was pointing to wasn't the same man who'd been staying at the B&B up until the day after Barry Golding died, this whole Innocore angle was something that needed more looking into.

"Is there any way to get a list of names for the people who worked for this company?" she asked me.

"I bet Ryan could. We need to tell him about this." I folded my arms and looked absently around the room. Cheryl had gone out to the porch and Maria sat close to Aunt Meg, comforting her. "Why don't you show him before he leaves? I have to get back to the kitchen. I've got too much to do. But definitely tell him. I'm sure he'd be interested. I know they're looking into the company too, but this seems like something important."

She nodded, and I gave her shoulder a squeeze. "You're right about the research. You're a master indeed. Good job."

Bertie swiveled in her chair and beamed at me. "I love it. So much fun. It's like solving a puzzle."

I knew just what she was talking about. Clearly, I couldn't get enough of solving crimes either.

Heading back to the kitchen, I pulled out the onions I'd been working on and went back to chopping as I thought. Another murder in the group. It had to be the same person who'd killed both Barry and Tori. And now there were only three possibilities, at least in *my* mind. It also had to be someone who knew about Tori's allergy, but I supposed that would probably be everyone she worked with. Tori had never been shy about stating her needs, and a peanut allergy would certainly be common knowledge in the group.

She must have gone looking for an epi pen as soon as she'd felt the effects, which is why the contents of her purse had been thrown everywhere. Whoever killed her had likely taken the pen from her purse before poisoning her with peanuts.

I let my mind wander through the possibilities as I finished the onions and started slicing zucchini, eggplant, and peppers to roast. The steady rhythm of my knife helped calm my nerves. A few times, Aunt Meg came in to check on me or to make coffee for Ryan and Ty. I tried to tune it all out and focus on my work. Despite what was happening around me, the party for sixty people sat heavy on my shoulders and I focused deeply on my job, barely registering the occasional interruptions.

Cassie flew through the door a little after five. "Ty called and told me what happened." Her eyes were enormous, and she seemed to be positively buzzing with energy. Cocoa hopped up from where he'd been napping under the table to greet her, his energy suddenly matching Cassie's. The two of them played for a minute and Cassie scratched behind his ears before coming to sit at the bar. Cocoa, realizing he wouldn't get more attention, resumed his napping post under the kitchen table.

"Did you find her body?"

I shook my head. "Maria. She was pretty upset, obviously."

"Do you have any thoughts about who did it?" she asked, her voice dropping lower.

I turned on the stove and put a massive skillet over the flame. I would partially cook the chicken breasts, set them into chafing dishes, and then bake them to doneness tomorrow morning and drizzle them with the lemon caper sauce at the very last minute. The oil in the pan sizzled, and I dipped the flattened chicken breasts in first flour, then egg mixture, and finally bread crumbs. "I don't know. It could have been any of the three of them." I told her about the peanut allergy and the smoothie. "My guess is somebody snuck in here and put peanuts into her acai. And then somehow got into her things and took the epi pen from her purse. Which is why she and her purse were both on the ground the way they were."

Cassie shivered. "That's awful. What a way to go." She registered all the work I was frantically doing. "You need any help?"

I shook my head. "Surprisingly, I feel pretty good right now. We'll see how I feel in the morning, though."

Cassie nodded and stood. "Alright, I'm gonna say hi to Ty if he's free and then I'm heading back home. I just wanted to come over and check on y'all. You staying long over here?"

I looked around the kitchen, trying to gauge how much more I could get done for the party ahead of time. "Yeah, probably another two or three hours at least. Don't wait for me for dinner."

She nodded and then reached over and squeezed my shoulder. I blew out a breath. "Don't worry, lady, you've got this. And we'll figure out what happened to Barry and Tori. This nightmare is going to be finished with before you know it."

I hoped she was right.

Chapter Twenty-One

The next morning I snuck into Primrose House as early as I dared. The sun was just peeking over the trees and the air held the faintest moisture from another rain in the night. All was quiet as I slipped inside through the kitchen door and hit the lights. First, I set breakfast out so Aunt Meg wouldn't have to do it. Then I pulled my apron on, ready to get to work. I would head over to Blanco around ten and finish all the cooking there, but I still had a mountain of prep work to do before then.

Eric surprised me a little while later. He came into the kitchen with his hair sticking every which way, his eyes swollen and bleary. "I thought I smelled coffee."

I motioned with my head toward the pot. "Just made it. Help yourself."

He glanced at the feta I was slicing and I could tell by the look that crossed his face that he was hungry. I caught his eye, and he gave me a lopsided smile. "Man, I could kill for an egg sandwich. You know any place that's open this early around here?"

I smiled and put the feta into a container. "If you give me ten minutes, I can make you one. Is ham and cheese okay too?"

His grin lit up his face. "Awesome."

I didn't really have time to waste, but I thought that maybe, just maybe, if I fed this young man, he might be willing to part with some information.

"Should I come back, or..." he said as he finished pouring himself a big mug of black coffee.

"No, it won't take long. Have a seat." If I let him go, I might not get anything out of him.

I pulled a package of country ham and sharp cheddar out of the fridge and then selected a nice puffy croissant from the breakfast tray Aunt Meg had prepared the night before for the B&B guests. I heated my pan with a little oil and waited, glancing at Eric and back again.

"You doing okay? I know you and Tori were...close."

He frowned and turned his cup around and around. "I can't believe she's dead. I know it was silly, but I really did like her." His voice caught, and he took a big swallow, nearly choking on the hot liquid.

I nodded and cracked an egg, the sizzle of it filling the emptiness in the room. "It sounded like you thought Kevin might be responsible," I gently prodded, hoping against hope he wouldn't think me overly nosy and clam up.

The kid looked out the window over the sink wistfully. "I thought he was the one who killed Barry. I told Kevin some things about Barry right before he died. Some things that made Kevin furious. So I thought it was him. I mean, who else would it have been? And you know, Tori might have found something out about it all. That could be why she died, too. I just hate to think it was all my fault."

"Why would it be your fault?" I flipped the egg quickly, cooking it for another few seconds before sliding it gently onto the sliced croissant. Next, I put the ham in the pan to warm through.

"Because if I'd never told Kevin about the old company, about what Barry did, he wouldn't have killed Barry. And he wouldn't have killed Tori."

Kevin chose that minute to walk into the kitchen. "Spreading lies again, Eric?"

Eric's face froze, his cheeks blazed, and his eyes darted around the room. He looked scared. "I'm just getting some breakfast."

"Why don't you keep your mouth shut? You don't need to be going around telling strangers our business."

The room crackled with tension. I hoped they wouldn't start fighting in my kitchen. I slid the ham onto the sandwich and topped it with cheese, then closed it up and handed it to Eric.

"Thanks," he said, grabbing the plate and fleeing the kitchen without another word.

Kevin poured himself a cup of coffee and took a lazy sip. "You people sure are nosy," he said as he watched me chopping through vegetables. "Could be dangerous for you if you aren't careful."

My cheeks flared, but he grabbed an apple from the bowl and left the kitchen before I could respond. Was that a threat? It sure felt like one. I had an overwhelming urge to call Ryan, but I held off, knowing he'd be here soon enough. He'd told me the day before that they planned on coming back this morning to finish looking through all the rooms. As of last night, they still had found no epi pens in the house, although they'd confirmed with the doctor that Tori did in fact have a deadly peanut allergy and she had a prescription for an epi pen.

Bertie came in a little while later. All my early morning guests were truly surprising. Usually I had the kitchen to myself until at least seven, but not today. Her eyes danced as she poured herself coffee and added a generous splash of cream. "The chef in her element," she said with a laugh. "Do you need me to help you out today?"

I glanced around, mentally processing everything I'd need to do and whether help would be welcome or whether showing a new person how to work a catering job would just slow me down. "I think I've got it, unless you really want to."

She smiled. "It seems fun, but Cassie invited me to go to that pre-look thingy for the estate sale with her. I've always wanted to see what's up with these estate sales. Might be something I try out back in Spoonbill Bay, so I think I'll go with her if you don't mind."

"Of course not! You should have fun while you're here. I'm sorry it's been such a downer of a trip for you so far!"

Bertie waved that away and got a gleam in her eye. "I told your boyfriend about our hunches yesterday before he left."

She waggled her eyebrows, and I laughed. "What did he say?"

"He said it was interesting and that they'd look into it. I emailed him the article and a couple of other things I found about the old company. Looks like they went under just after Barry left, about two years ago. It was a surprise to a lot of people because it was supposed to be some hot new technology and the company had a lot of potential before it tanked."

I puzzled over it as I whipped up a massive bowl of lava cake batter. I'd need two of the bowls to make enough lava cakes for the crowd. My arm ached with all the stirring.

"We'll have to ask him if they found anything when he comes over. I think they're going to do another round of interviews with the group today. Ryan told me it was indeed the acai that was tampered with by the way. Crushed up peanuts in the bag. So somebody definitely had it out for Tori."

"It's only one of three, so it shouldn't be too hard to figure out."

I frowned, remembering the veiled threat from Kevin just a few minutes before. "My bet is on Kevin. I could have seen Eric killing Barry, but the kid was smitten with Tori. There's no way he would have killed her."

"What about Cheryl?"

Pausing my stirring, I pulled out the first of the muffin tins I would use for the lava cakes and poured the batter in, then thought for a minute. "I doubt it. I know she was in the bathroom when Barry fell, so she couldn't have killed him. And if she killed Tori, then we're looking at two killers and that's just way too complicated. Especially for such a small group."

Bertie nodded and sipped her coffee. "That's what I thought too. I wonder how much Tori knew about all this Innocore business. You think she could have died because she figured out the secret, and from that, also figured out who killed Barry?"

"That's my guess. It makes the most sense. The only other thing I can think of is that either Kevin or Cheryl found out about Barry and Tori plotting to take off with the money. Maybe Kevin or Cheryl killed both of them to protect the company."

"Or maybe Eric killed them both for the same reason. He found out they were planning to run away together and jealousy got the best of him."

"It's possible. But he sure is broken up about Tori dying."

"It could be an act," she mused.

I nodded. "Maybe, but I'd be pretty surprised. He doesn't seem like the type. Although I haven't known him for more than a week so my judgement of his character isn't based on much."

Scraping the last of the lava cake batter into the final muffin tin, I covered them all with a healthy amount of plastic wrap so they wouldn't get spilled when I took them over to Blanco. I glanced at the clock and fretted when I realized it was nearly eight. Bertie and I had talked for almost an hour. I had about one hour left to prep, and then it was time to pack everything up in the car. It was the one unknown that I was really dreading. Could I actually fit everything in? Blanco was about half an hour's drive, so if I had to make two trips to make it work, it would really cut into cooking time. And that was time I could not afford to lose.

Before I could think any more about lost time, Ryan stepped into the kitchen in his uniform. His boots clinked on the tile and he moved in quickly to me to give me a kiss. He laughed and wiped a drop of chocolate batter off my face, and I blushed.

"Good morning, ladies," he said as he moved away from me and back into sheriff mode. His eyes danced and I could tell he had good news.

"Bertie. Just the lady I was looking for. I wanted to let you know first. That info you found yesterday? It was extremely helpful. After doing a whole lot of digging, we did indeed find an employee list for Innocore Solutions. And it turns out that the man you thought looked familiar was Jeff Hildebrand."

We both gasped. It was the same name the man who'd checked in with his wife last Friday had used. "Is it the couple, then?"

He nodded. "Looks that way, although we still need to question them. It's quite the coincidence, though. I'd be shocked if it turned out that he wasn't responsible for Mr. Golding's death. We've been in touch with the San Francisco police force and they've detained them both already."

"Not San Diego?"

He shook his head. "Looks like that was the only thing he lied about. The woman was indeed his wife, and it was indeed their anniversary. He didn't even use an alias. He must have been confident that he would get away with it. Or too clueless to bother with a lie."

The news was an absolute shock. Bertie and I stared at each other, dumbfounded.

"But how did he know Barry was going to be here in Texas? And why choose now to kill him? What was his motive?"

"We're looking into all that still, and I don't have a lot of answers. We just broke the case about an hour ago, thanks to Bertie's information. And yours, of course," he glanced at me with a quick smile. "As far as we can tell, the technology that Barry stole from Innocore to start his new company was created by Jeff Hildebrand. So he was probably out for revenge. From what we learned, it seems to be a very lucrative technology."

I nodded. That went along with what we found out. "But what about Tori? Tori died *after* they left."

Ryan frowned and crossed his arms. "Honestly, I'm not sure. Maybe the deaths aren't related, although that's also quite a coincidence." He looked out the window and then back at me with a smile. "We've still got a lot of work to do, obviously, but we're making some significant progress now. Alright, I just wanted to let you both know the good news. I'm going to get back to interviewing these people, see if we can work out the rest of the puzzle." He leaned over for another kiss.

"Well, isn't that a load of excitement? I didn't need my coffee this morning after all!" Bertie said with a laugh. Giving her a smile, I pulled all of my catering gear together. I'd called yesterday afternoon to make sure the convention center had dishes and silver for the event, but I still needed to take everything I'd need for cooking and serving the buffet. It was a massive amount of supplies, but as usual, I'd made an exhaustive list to check off so I wouldn't forget anything.

"How strange to think that someone killed Tori, too. I wonder if it's related to Barry's death?" I mused as I added spoons and bags to the growing pile.

"Maybe someone thought Barry's death was a convenient cover to get rid of Tori? Maybe someone wanted her dead for another reason and got lucky with an excuse when Barry died?"

It was an interesting idea. One that I would have to think about. But not right now. All thoughts of murder and motives would have to wait until after my event.

"Alright," I told Bertie. "It's pretty much go-time for me. Sorry to have to leave you to do the sleuthing and puzzling on your own, but I've got to get going. Maria is always great with this stuff, though. She should be in shortly. Make sure to tell her about the couple. She's gonna be so surprised!"

"No problemo. Good luck today!" She came around and gave me a big squeeze. I could feel the excitement course through her and I remembered how it felt when I'd figured out that first murder back in April. The high of doing something so important and so difficult had been intoxicating. I could just imagine what Bertie was feeling at the moment, knowing her master research skills had led Ryan to the probable answer of who killed Barry Golding.

If only we knew who'd killed Tori. But that puzzle would have to wait until after I fed the Blanco Audubon Society.

Chapter Twenty-Two

To say that packing everything to feed sixty people into a Honda coupe is a tight squeeze is a serious understatement. The backseat and trunk of my car were a jigsaw puzzle of coolers, trays, and utensils, each piece Tetris-ed in with the kind of precision that would make an engineer weep. I was so thankful they had a kitchen and dishes ready for me at the event space. If they hadn't, I might have had to serve salad out of a hat and hope nobody noticed.

It took me longer than I'd expected to get everything into the car, so when I finally pulled out of the parking lot of Primrose House near ten, I pushed the pedal to the metal and hoped to make up for lost time on the highway.

And there I was, puttering along on the highway as fast as I could go, my little Honda packed to the gills, when the unexpected soundtrack of my catering adventure took a turn for the dramatic. A horrible screeching noise erupted from the car—like a banshee with a bad attitude—followed by a worrying clicking. Then, no matter how hard I pumped the gas pedal, my car responded with the enthusiasm of a stubborn mule refusing to budge.

Shoot.

I coasted to the side of the road, coming to a stop with a series of bumps and jolts. Sitting there on the edge of the highway, the reality of my situation set in. Huge big rigs thundered by, each one shaking my little car like a maraca in a salsa band. I couldn't help but laugh at the absurdity of it all. Here I was, trying to pull off a catering miracle, and now I was stranded on the side of the road with a car full of food and an engine that had apparently taken early retirement.

I pulled out my phone, fingers crossed for a signal strong enough to call for help. Meanwhile, I started mentally rearranging my plans. The menu might need to become a bit more... avant-garde, depending on how long I was stuck here. "Roadside Chic," I'd call it. A new culinary trend, inspired by necessity and a broken-down Honda.

Wanting to cry, but knowing it wouldn't magically fix my car, I scrolled through my contacts and frowned. Cassie and Bertie were on their picking adventure. Aunt Meg was hosting her own version of a thriller at the B&B, and my usual go-tos, Mark and Sheila, were nowhere near town. I chewed my lip, my mind racing for alternatives. Finally, with great reluctance, I realized what my only option was. I sighed.

With a heavy heart, I dialed Ryan, and he picked up right away.

"Hey, Ryan. I know you're probably swamped, and I hate to bother you, but... I'm stranded." I explained the dire situation, my looming deadline for the Blanco event, and how, at this moment, I felt like nothing could get any worse. "It's okay if you can't help," I added, although I didn't really mean it.

"Where are you? I'll be right there," Ryan's voice cut through my defeat, sharp and decisive. Guilt gnawed at me for pulling him from his duties, but mostly I was mighty relieved. I was stuck between a rock and a hard place, and he was my only way out.

As soon as Ryan's cruiser rolled up, his face was a mix of worry and determination. "You weren't kidding about the 'little bit stranded' part," he remarked as he got out of the car, scanning the overloaded Honda with a raised eyebrow.

"Yeah, it's like a culinary clown car," I admitted, trying to keep the mood light despite the sinking feeling in my stomach. Together, we started the precarious task of transferring the catering supplies and food into his much larger vehicle.

"I haven't played Tetris with food before," Ryan joked, as he carefully wedged a cooler between the front seat and the back.

"I owe you big time for this," I said, watching him work magic with the space. "Dinner's on me for a month."

"Only a month?" he teased, closing the trunk with a satisfied thud. "I was thinking this kind of rescue deserves at least a two-month dinner subscription."

I held a bowl of pasta on my lap as we sped through the countryside. The good thing about having a sheriff pick you up after being stranded is that he can get you where you need to go in one-half less than no time at all. The siren cleared out whatever cars were in our way and we made it to downtown Blanco in less than ten minutes.

As the cruiser pulled up to the Blanco Convention Hall, I saw several elderly women standing around the front of the building. They stopped and stared at us. I took a deep breath and steeled my nerves before getting out of the car. I couldn't imagine anything more ridiculous than a caterer showing up at an event in a police car.

What a life I was living.

Ryan grabbed three pans of chicken out of the trunk with ease and waited for me to slide the uncooked lava cakes out of the backseat as carefully as I could. At least his car had more room than mine. Not that I was planning on making this a regular thing, but it was nice to not have everything so cramped. He followed me up to the front, where the women still stood watching us.

I took a deep breath, readying myself for the whirlwind I was about to step into. "Hi, there. I'm Abby with Deep in the Heart

Catering. I'm catering this afternoon's lunch. Do you happen to know where Maribeth Rogers is?"

A woman, towering above the rest, peered down at me with a mixture of curiosity and hospitality. "She's inside. Probably in the kitchen. I'll show you the way," she said, her tone suggesting this was the most excitement they'd seen in a while. She headed for the front door and the rest of the women all followed behind us, unwilling to let this adventure pass them by.

As we navigated through the gathered crowd, I noticed their glances shifting between me and Ryan, their curiosity piqued by the sheriff turned catering assistant. The whispers and nudges did not escape me, but the questions brewing in their eyes would have to remain a mystery, at least for now.

We threaded our way through the bustling hall, the sound of preparations and quiet chatter filling the air. As we entered the kitchen, I sighed with relief. It was a sanctuary amidst the chaos, small and utilitarian but bathed in the comforting glow of natural light from skylights above. My eyes quickly took stock of the appliances—commercial-grade ovens that promised efficiency and reliability and two large refrigerators. Exactly what I needed.

The woman leading the way announced our presence. "Maribeth, these people are looking for you."

The woman who turned to greet us had the kind of warm, welcoming smile that immediately put you at ease. "Oh, hello there. You must be Abby," the woman said. "I'm Maribeth Rogers. And hello to you, Sheriff," Maribeth's mouth crept up in a smile, her eyes flicking between Ryan and me, a spark of intrigue lighting up her gaze.

The moment was brief, a bit of friendly chatter before we dove into the task at hand. But it was enough to remind me why I loved this job—each event a new adventure, each challenge an opportunity to create something memorable.

She waved to the kitchen. "Make yourself at home. Once you get settled in, I'll show you the dining room."

Ryan and I headed back out to the cruiser after we found two massive carts, which would make unloading much easier. We both took the job seriously and worked as fast as we dared. There wasn't any time to waste, not for either of us. I had an event to cater, and he had a murder... or two... to solve.

As we finally finished unloading everything, Ryan smiled and gave me a quick hug, catching me off guard when he asked, "what time should I come and get you?" His voice was casual, but I could sense the underlying concern.

I fumbled for a response, my cheeks warming with a blush. I hadn't even thought about how I'd get home after the event. Getting to the event was the only thing on my mind. Until that point, at least. "Oh, I don't think you have to pick me up. I'll figure something out." The very idea of inconveniencing him further made me uneasy, even though his presence had been my lifeline today.

But Ryan was having none of it. "Abby, honey. I want to come and get you. I would be upset if you asked anyone else. That's what a boyfriend is for, after all. Among other things," he added, his voice dropping to a softer, more intimate tone. He glanced around quickly and then gave me a tender kiss.

In that moment, standing amid pots and pans and chaos, I realized how lucky I was to have someone like Ryan in my life. His support, unwavering even when I was knee deep in catering madness, was the kind of stuff you read about in romance novels but rarely find in real life.

"Okay," I finally agreed, my voice a whisper, still caught up in the warmth of his kiss. "You can come get me. Maybe around two? I'll text you if it's any different."

"If something happens and I can't make it back, I'll send Ty. But barring any emergencies, I'll be here."

Watching Ryan disappear through the side door sent an unexpected flutter through my heart, but sentimentality would have to take a back seat for now. There was a feast to be orchestrated.

Springing into action, I channeled my inner kitchen warrior, putting all the food into the fridge or the oven, and then set up the chafing dishes in the hall where lunch would be served. I found a rhythm after only a few minutes of fumbling. It's funny how a car breakdown could throw me for a loop, but give me a kitchen crisis, and I find my stride in no time at all. Self-pity was a luxury I couldn't afford, not with the clock ticking and hungry guests on the horizon.

The next hour zipped by in a blur of steam and spices, and as I finally stepped back to survey my handiwork after placing the last chafing dish full of food in its holder, a sense of pride swelled within me. fruits of my labor, ready to be devoured.

The doors opened, and the men and women of the Blanco Audubon Society streamed in, their plates soon heaping with my culinary creations. Watching them, I felt a mix of relief and exhilaration. Despite the hurdles, the feast was ready, and my heart, still fluttering with thoughts of Ryan, knew that today, I'd managed to pull off something special.

Midway through the bustling event, as I busied myself topping up the pasta and vegetables, a snippet of conversation caught my ear, slicing through the hum of chatter like a knife through butter.

"Hey, isn't that the caterer who poisoned somebody in Sugar Creek a while back? Don't eat any more of the food, Charles!" The tone was half-joking, half-wary, and it pinged off my irritation like a well-aimed dart.

Rolling my eyes, I couldn't believe my ears. Of all the reputations to precede me into Blanco, it had to be this one. Not my knack for turning a last-minute catering gig into a feast or my ability to juggle dishes with the finesse of a circus performer, but a wildly inaccurate tale of culinary crime.

"That's a misconception," I interjected, striving to keep my voice light and infused with a humor I didn't quite feel. "I was actually the one who figured out who *did* poison those people." The words tumbled out, part correction, part plea for a little faith.

They shot me skeptical looks, their eyes darting between the food and me as if expecting me to whip out a vial of poison then and there. I plastered on my best 'trustworthy caterer' smile, trying to radiate innocence and culinary competence in equal measure.

Other than the minor run-in, the event unfolded smoother than a well-oiled skillet from that point on. The lava cakes, in particular, were a hit, their centers as molten as my determination to prove my worth beyond the whispers of scandal. Each one was a little victory, a testament to the magic that happens when you bake with both precision and a pinch of defiance. I mentally book-marked the recipe, a secret weapon in my arsenal for when I needed a showstopper.

As the last guest left, their taste buds undoubtedly singing, Maribeth Rogers sought me out amidst my cleanup crusade. Her words were like the cherry on top of an already rewarding day. "Thank you so much, I cannot tell you how grateful I am that you were able to make this work, lava cakes and all!"

Flashing her my most genuine caterer's smile, I replied, "Oh, it's my pleasure, ma'am. I appreciate your business, and spreading the word about Deep in the Heart Catering would be the icing on the cake for me."

As I packed up my gear, the satisfaction of a job well-done buoying my spirits, I couldn't help but think about the road ahead. With every satisfied customer, I was slowly but surely seasoning my reputation with success, one event at a time. And as I looked forward to the adventures awaiting in the next chapter, I knew one thing for sure: in the world of catering, there would never be predictability.

Chapter Twenty-Three

When Ryan pulled up right at two in his personal pickup truck, a beast that made my tiny Honda look like a toy, I did a little happy dance. The pile of equipment that needed to return to the B&B seemed to have multiplied when I wasn't looking, looming like a culinary Everest and I was so grateful for all the space in the back as we piled the bed high with catering odds and ends.

Climbing into the truck beside him after we got everything settled, I let out a sigh that carried the weight of the day. My muscles ached, and my brain felt like it had been through a blender set to 'puree.'

"I can't thank you enough for helping me," I said, buckling my seatbelt as he started the engine. The familiar rumble under me was comforting, especially when I thought about the absolute silence of my own traitorous vehicle.

Ryan shot me a look that was all warmth and amusement. "What are boyfriends for if not for rescue missions?" His tone was light, but sincere and tinged with concern. And there was that boyfriend word again. I was surprised he was so comfortable throwing it around since we hadn't really talked about what we were to each other yet. But I liked it, I liked it a lot.

I leaned my head back in the seat as the truck rolled out onto the road, taking us back to Sugar Creek and away from the adventure of the day.

Outside the window, the landscape whizzed by, a blur of greens and browns as we left Blanco behind. I sunk deeper into the seat, exhaustion seeping into my bones, but a small smile played on my lips. Despite the car trouble, the last-minute job, and the physical toll, there was a part of me that thrived on the chaos.

"I think we make a pretty good team," I mused out loud, half to Ryan, half to myself.

"I agree, honey," he said.

"Were you able to make any more progress on figuring out what happened with Tori?" I asked.

He leaned over the steering wheel, one hand lazily guiding us down the highway. "Nothing much yet, although we found two epi pens in a bag in the trash bins behind Primrose House, so I am absolutely certain now the allergic reaction and her death were premeditated."

I frowned and closed my eyes. "Well, we only have three choices at this point. So it shouldn't be too hard to figure out. One of the three of them did it, right?"

"Unless one of y'all killed her," he replied. My eyes flew open, and I smacked his thigh when I saw the smirk on his face. "Yes, without a doubt. One of the three remaining employees killed Tori. And thanks to the San Francisco police department, we're sure that Jeff Hildebrand killed Barry."

My eyebrows shot up. "Wow! How'd they figure that out?"

"He confessed. Said he came to Sugar Creek to kill Barry, that he found out from a press release that they would be in town and figured killing him in Texas would make it harder to solve the crime. He went to Wild Hare the day before and pulled the screws out of that rail when nobody was looking. So we've got a solid confession. That part, at least, is solved. The problem of Tori's death, though…that is still very much up in the air."

"Wow. That's great news. Good for them, that they got a confession so quickly. And I'm glad to know Mark and Sheila weren't responsible in any way." I sat up suddenly as I realized where we were. "Hey, wait a minute!" I exclaimed, a mix of confusion and sudden realization dawning on me as I noticed we'd breezed right past the turnoff for Sugar Creek at least five minutes ago. "Where are you taking me?"

Ryan's smirk got even bigger, and it made me super nervous suddenly. "We're going shopping," he said, his voice filled with excitement. My heart sank. I did not like surprises, especially after I'd already had so many on this endless day.

"What?" The word escaped me like a startled bird.

"You need a new car, and you need one now," he continued, as if he'd just stated the world's most obvious fact.

"Oh no, I don't," I countered, my immediate reflex to resist change with all the force of my being. The thought of shopping for a car, with all its implications and commitments, was too much too soon.

"Yes, you do." Ryan was unyielding, his tone brokering no argument. "While you were working, I had Micah from the garage I use stop by and look. Your car," he paused for dramatic effect, "is beyond help. The engine's more or less a glorified paperweight now. Fixing it would cost thousands. Certainly more than the car's worth."

I wanted to argue. But I was sure they were right. Still, I didn't have the funds for this. Not to mention, I needed time to wrap my head around it all before making such a big decision.

Despite my protests, we pulled into the used car dealership a few minutes later. Cars and trucks in a variety of conditions filled the lot.

As we stepped out of the truck, I took a deep breath, trying to channel some of Ryan's apparent confidence about this excursion.

A man came out of the dealership a minute later and swooped in with the grace of a vulture spotting its next meal. "Welcome to Joe's Quality Used Cars! I'm Joe, and I'll be helping you find the perfect vehicle today!" His smile was as slick as his hair, oozing a kind of enthusiasm that set my teeth on edge.

But the moment his eyes landed on Ryan's uniform, the transformation was almost comical. The sheen of confidence dimmed, replaced by equal measures respect and wariness. "Oh, Sheriff, didn't realize y'all were in the market for a new vehicle."

"We're not," Ryan clarified with a nod towards me, "but she is."

As Joe took us around toward the back of the lot, my eyes caught sight of it—a commercial van that seemed made for my catering dreams. I leaned in to look in the window and saw it was spacious, with enough room to transport even the most elaborate of setups.

But then I saw the price tag, and my heart sank. It was perfect, but it was also leagues beyond what I could afford.

Ryan came over and pulled the side door open. "Wow, this is exactly what you need!"

"It's not gonna happen," I told him, crossing my arms with a frown.

"What do you mean? This is the perfect catering van," Ryan replied.

"I can't afford it right now!" I gritted my teeth, the words tasting bitter. I felt bad for being short with him, but as the dream of seamlessly carting my culinary creations without fearing a breakdown seemed to evaporate before my eyes and it made me downright angry.

Ryan straightened and turned to me, his expression earnest, bordering on adamant. "Look, I can't stand the idea of you driving that hunk of junk you currently own. Even if you could get it fixed, there's no guarantee it'll stay safe. What if I'm not able to help you next time? What if it leads to you getting hurt?"

He put his hands on his hips and frowned. "I want you to take a loan from me, and I don't want you to argue. I need to know you're gonna be safe, honey. I care about you too much to let you jeopardize yourself in that way."

The words hung in the air between us, heavy with implications. Borrowing money was a line I hated to cross, especially from a man I was dating. It could get messy, fast. Yet, looking into Ryan's eyes, seeing the genuine concern and the unspoken promise of support, I found my resolve wavering. This wasn't just about a van or money; it was about safety, about planning for a future where my business—and I—wouldn't be at the mercy of an unreliable vehicle.

"Okay," I finally said, the word barely a whisper. It was a concession, but also an acknowledgment of the partnership we were building, one where pride took a backseat to practicality and care.

We cosigned the paperwork in Joe's office a few minutes later and he told me he'd call me to pick the van up just as soon as the loan cleared, which would probably be the next day. Despite all the guilt I felt about the new van, I was pretty darn excited about it, too, now that the deed was done.

As we walked back to Ryan's truck, I was filled with gratitude and apprehension. Life in Sugar Creek was never dull, but with Ryan by my side, it seemed even the bumpiest of roads could lead to new beginnings.

We barely talked on the way back to Primrose House. I was reeling from all that had happened, embarrassed that Ryan had had to bail me out of my car troubles, especially when he was in the middle of a murder investigation. It was exciting to know that I finally had a proper catering truck, but daunting to think about how much I owed the dealership and Ryan, too. It would take a lot of catering to repay them.

When we finally got back to the B&B, we each grabbed a chafing dish and headed inside. I wanted to get the truck unloaded fast so Ryan could get back to work. We found Bertie and Aunt Meg in the kitchen cleaning up dinner dishes when we came into the kitchen a few minutes later.

"Well, here she is!" Aunt Meg said. "I was getting worried about you! I thought your event ended at two and here it is after dinner."

My cheeks flushed. With all the excitement, I'd forgotten to call and check in. "Sorry, I had some car trouble. Ryan came and rescued me and then we stopped by a dealership on the way home —not my idea—," I glanced at Ryan and he grinned. "And now you're looking at the brand new owner of a commercial catering van!"

"Oh, that is such good news!" Aunt Meg told me with a hug. "And I sure am grateful to you, Ryan, for rescuing our girl and helping her see the light on a new vehicle."

"I want to see it!" Bertie said. "How exciting!"

"The financing and paperwork are still going through so I don't have it yet, but we can go pick it up tomorrow sometime. You can come then and ride home with me!"

Together, Ryan and I finished unloading the truck quickly without saying much of anything. I think he knew I needed time alone to process everything that happened, and I appreciated his willingness to give it to me.

"Thank you," I said as we finally finished, the darkness beginning to settle in around us. My words were inadequate to express the depth of my appreciation. "I don't know how I can ever repay you for today."

Ryan gave me a sweet smile and pulled me into him. "Just keep cooking amazing food and making Sugar Creek a tastier place. That's payment enough for me." His gaze shifted, a hint of reluctance to leave mingling with the duty that called him back. "I've got to head back to the station, but I'll call you later, okay?"

"Okay," I replied, suddenly not wanting to let him go.

He bent to kiss me, and I wrapped my hands around his neck,

pulling him in closer. We leaned into each other for a moment and I closed my eyes. It had been a monumental day between Ryan rescuing me on the road, the thrill and grind of the catering event, and the excitement and fear and reliance on Ryan that buying a new vehicle had brought my way. I would need a long time to recuperate and process.

The one thing I knew, though, as I watched Ryan pull out of the Primrose House parking lot, was that I was one lucky woman. To have such a wonderful man who wanted to call himself my boyfriend did a lot to bolster me. Turning back to the B&B, I thought of Aunt Meg and Bertie and Maria and Cassie all in my corner too and knew I was truly blessed to have so much love and care all around me. L.A. could never be a match for that. If only I'd known it before I'd ever left Sugar Creek.

But some lessons are ones that have to be learned the hard way.

Chapter Twenty-Four

Wednesday morning I woke up more sore than a hyena at a comedy club. But there was a spring in my step as soon as I remembered my new van. I used it as motivating fuel to make it past the pain and get out of bed. I also realized that today was Aunt Meg's birthday. We wouldn't be able to have a party for her, but I was going to try my hardest to make it a good day anyway, and to make her feel special.

Making a few quick calls after I showered and ate a bowl of oatmeal, I got someone to tow the old Honda over to the used car lot. Joe, the used salesman, had said he'd give me a fair deal on a trade-in, even with the engine problem. Normally I wouldn't have trusted him for a second, but he'd seemed thoroughly persuaded toward honesty by Ryan's sheriff uniform.

I debated waiting for a day before taking samples around to potential business clients, but I had some leftover ingredients from the party prep that I could use and I wanted to capitalize on the excitement I still had from the job I'd finished the day before. After a quick store trip, I was back on the road toward Primrose House.

For the first time since the California group had arrived nearly a week ago, the B&B felt deserted when I walked in midmorning. The front room was empty, and I didn't hear a single raised voice. I wandered down the hall and poked my head in the dining room—empty, too. The entire house was shrouded in an unfamiliar quiet that sent shivers down my spine. Puzzled by the silence, I wandered through the house after putting away the groceries, searching for Aunt Meg and Bertie but finding no sign of either one of them. Finally, I stumbled on them sitting out at the picnic table on the side of the house.

"Happy birthday, Aunt Meg!" I cried as I saw her. I rushed over and gave her a big hug, nearly knocking her off her seat. She laughed and patted my arm, then the seat beside her. I slid in with a smile.

"What are you two up to out here?" I asked.

Aunt Meg's smile faded and her face showed fatigue, her usually vibrant demeanor replaced by a haggard exhaustion I hadn't seen in years. It pained me to see her so worn down.

"Just enjoying the morning," Bertie replied, her tone light, attempting to change the heavy mood.

"You okay, Aunt Meg?"

She sighed and nodded, but didn't meet my gaze. "It's hard to sleep knowing there's a killer in the house."

Bertie glanced worriedly at her cousin and steered the conversation in a new direction. "What about you? What's on your agenda today?"

I paused, not sure I wanted to let Aunt Meg's worries drop, but I wasn't sure what to say to make her feel better either. Shrugging, I said, "I thought I'd go ahead with the sample idea I had. Take some sandwiches and things around lunchtime to the businesses downtown. I've got a little cooking to do, but nothing too serious. Not like yesterday, at least." I paused, remembering another task. "I also need to pick up my new van sometime today! Maybe one of you could drive me, if you don't mind. It's at that used dealership just off the highway, Joe's. Not too far from here."

Aunt Meg's smile was a small light in the dim morning. "Of course, honey. I'd be happy to."

"I was also thinking we could all go out to dinner tonight, or get takeout from Lulu's or something, if that sounds better. I know we can't have a party, but we've got to celebrate somehow!"

Aunt Meg nodded and smiled. "That would be nice. But nothing too fancy, and I don't want you cooking! I think we could all use a break." She had me there. As it was, I would be lucky if I had enough energy to do the samples.

Seeking to catch up on any developments I might have missed, I ventured, "has anything new happened around here since last night?"

Bertie and Aunt Meg both shook their heads. "It's been eerily quiet, to tell the truth. I thought I wanted the quiet, but the quiet makes me even more nervous," Aunt Meg confessed, her voice dropping to a whisper. "Especially since one of them is a killer. Gives me the heebie-jeebies."

Bertie chimed in with her usual spunk, "I'd be out of here in a jiffy if it wasn't for Meg here. What kind of cousin would I be if I left her alone with these nuts?"

I laughed and shrugged.

Aunt Meg waved away the concern with a flick of her hand. "Oh, shoo. Please! You know I can take care of myself, Bert."

"Oh, I know it! But what fun would it be to leave? I was only joking. I want to stick around to see what happens! I feel invested in this thing now that I'm a part of the investigation," Bertie said with a laugh, the tension briefly lifting. "Speaking of which, did you hear anything new from Ryan about Tori's death?"

"Nothing much. He's still looking into the background of everyone, but nothing new has come up yet. Not that I know of, at least," I replied. I'd told them all about Jeff Hildebrand and the epi pens the night before, so they were as caught up as I was.

Leaving them to their coffee and chitchat, I headed back inside, my thoughts already turning to my cooking plans. The brief exchange had made me uncomfortable more than anything. What an odd situation we'd all found ourselves in. I wondered how it would all come to an end. We needed to get rid of the drama, and needed to do it fast.

But for now, there were samples to prepare and a new van to pick up. Life, with all its mysteries and daily tasks, went on.

The sun poured in through the kitchen windows as I pulled out my cutting board and sharpened my favorite knife. I hoped it would be a productive day. I had a lot riding on these samples and I planned to give the food my best.

I decided on gourmet sandwiches and cherry crumb bars—each chosen for their potential to dazzle taste buds and showcase the best of what I could offer. I would slice the assortment of sandwiches—roasted vegetable with herbed goat cheese on ciabatta and turkey and cranberry chutney on seed bread—into small bites that could be easily passed around.

When Maria entered the kitchen a few minutes later, I was practically drowning in a sea of sandwiches. "Good morning," she greeted, her voice cutting through the flurry of my preparations. "How are you?"

"Well, nobody's died yet today, so I'm pretty good," I said, chuckling. Sometimes, you just have to find the humor in things.

Maria laughed too, the sound bright in the cluttered kitchen. "That's a good thing. Do you know where Meg is?"

As if summoned by the mention of her name, Aunt Meg and Bertie strolled in through the side door at that very moment.

"Oh good," Maria exclaimed, her face lighting up with a smile. She reached into her bag, pulling out a surprise. "I have something for you."

She carefully unveiled the blue and gold vase that the group had destroyed over the weekend. Now, it was miraculously whole again, its fractures filled with a lovely gold shimmer where Maria had painstakingly repaired it.

"I tried something I found online, a Japanese technique called kintsugi. It's traditionally done with genuine gold, but I managed to get a similar effect using superglue and acrylic paint." Her eyes were hopeful, almost shy, as she presented the mended piece. "I hope it's okay that I did this. I know it isn't the same anymore, but I thought it would be better than throwing it away, no?"

The vase, now gleaming with its gold-veined repairs, was now a display of the resilience and beauty in imperfection. Maria's thoughtful gesture was a good reminder that sometimes things broken could be put back together in ways that made them even more beautiful than before. It was an idea that hit home with all of us in that kitchen.

Tears welled up in Aunt Meg's eyes as she pulled Maria into a heartfelt hug. "It's beautiful. I'll cherish it always," she whispered, her voice thick with emotion.

I wasn't one bit surprised by Maria's gesture. She had many creative talents that she often kept hidden, like treasures waiting to be discovered. Her photography, for instance, was nothing short of phenomenal, bordering on artist quality. I still remembered a photo she'd shown me of her daughter Daniela amidst a sprawling field of lavender. The way she'd captured the essence of the moment, the emotions, and the play of light was so breathtaking that I found myself momentarily lost in the image when I first saw it.

The vase Aunt Meg now held felt the same. It was pretty before, but with its gold embellishment, it was captivating now, and held a story and a message.

As Aunt Meg and Bertie marveled at Maria's handiwork, I turned my attention back to the tasks in front of me. I mixed together the butter, sugar, and flour for the shortbread until it came together and then pressed it into a casserole dish.

I smiled as I watched the women leaning close into one another and talking. Maria's thoughtful gift and the shared moment it sparked had significantly lightened the mood from what it had been when I'd arrived and had made Aunt Meg's birthday just a little bit special. In the midst of our unexpected trials, it was these instances of connection and understanding that shone the brightest and I knew Aunt Meg would never forget Maria's thoughtful gesture.

After they left the kitchen, I focused all my attention on finishing the cherry crumb bars. They were bright, tangy, and sweet, with a buttery shortbread crust. Not only did they taste like a bite of summer, but they also held up well in a lunch box presentation, making them the perfect finale to my sample menu.

Cheryl came into the kitchen as I was boxing up the sandwich samples a while later and grabbed a bottle of water out of the small drink fridge in the corner. She eyed my cooking mess with a raised eyebrow. "Do you always cook here?"

I nodded. "This is the commercial kitchen I use for my catering business. Meg is my aunt, so she doesn't mind, but I pay her to use the space, too."

She nodded and tipped the water bottle back to take a deep drink. I caught sight of a bracelet on her wrist that had the initials *CHM*.

"Oh, does your middle name start with H? That's unusual. What is it?"

"No, H. is my maiden name."

She left without another word. I guess the group had moved from animosity and anger to the cold treatment. Worked for me. I had other things to think about at present.

I got the call that my loan had been approved and my new van was ready for pickup as I was pulling the bars out of the oven. I jumped up and down and screeched, overwhelmed by the excitement of finally having a van for my business. It was long overdue, and I felt bad for the fuss I'd made with Ryan the day before. I hated owing him, but in the end, it made everything much better.

My plan was to finish up the samples, clean myself up a little, gather all my fliers and cards and such, and then go pick up the van. I would stop back here and pack everything up, then head downtown. If only my van already had my logo on it. But that was an expensive step that would have to wait until a few more jobs came in.

I went around the house and found Bertie and Aunt Maria on the front porch, sipping tea and swinging on the porch swing. "It's time to pick up my van!"

Aunt Meg decided to stay and monitor the guests, so Bertie ran inside to get her keys and take me to Joe's lot. A few minutes later, we were in her SUV, heading down the highway.

"It must be pretty exciting having the sheriff for a boyfriend. I bet you hear all kinds of crazy stories," she said as she concentrated on the road.

I laughed. "Unfortunately, I'm very often the cause of the crazy stories."

She laughed too. "I bet he likes it. Gives a sense of excitement to y'all's relationship."

It was true, to a point. There was nothing quite as exciting to me as when Ryan got that frustrated glare in his eye. "So what really happened last night? Why does Aunt Meg seem so down today?"

Bertie shrugged. "Nothing really happened. The three who're left mostly kept to themselves but the tension of the house, boy. It's really uncomfortable. I think that's why she's so down."

"I know Ryan is working as hard as he can on this thing, but there's got to be something we can do to help him!" I said, the frustration of the situation really irking me. Not only did I want Aunt Meg's B&B to go back to normal, I wanted to find a way to repay Ryan for all his kindness. If I could help solve this murder business, maybe it would help.

"Well, we'll certainly keep our eyes out. We've done quite a bit already, but I know what you're saying. What we really need to do is figure out who killed Tori, and then we can get everything back to normal. Have a party for our girl."

As she said it, we pulled into the used car lot and I beamed. My van was sitting right by the front office, sparkling and clean, ready to take on its new life as a noble steed to Deep in the Heart Catering.

Chapter Twenty-Five

I was downright giddy as I pulled my van into the Primrose House parking lot a little before noon. Maria, Aunt Meg, and Bertie all came out to have a look, and I showed them the spacious back as I quickly loaded it with my samples. The space felt cavernous after having to make it work with other vehicles for the last few months and I giggled a little at the thrill of it all. The women wished me luck as I headed out for my very first adventure in my new van.

Driving downtown, I turned the radio up and drummed on the steering wheel. Things were looking up for my little business.

My first stop was to the small technical school just off the highway. I knew they hosted frequent events—dinners for alumni, gatherings for visiting speakers—not to mention all the employees whose personal celebrations might just be in need of my catering.

Finding a spot in the visitor's parking, I switched off the engine and took a moment to gather myself, drawing a deep, steadying breath. I was confident of my culinary creations, but the prospect of selling myself was not something I looked forward to. I'd always found comfort in the kitchen, behind the scenes. Stepping into the spotlight was a different challenge all together.

Navigating the bustling halls of the technical school with boxes of food was nerve-wracking, but after what seemed an age, I located the front office. There, I found the office manager, whose attention I needed to capture with my pitch.

"Good morning," I said. Looking at the nameplate, I took a deep breath and conjured my warmest smile. "Ms. Linden, I'm Abby Hirsch and I recently started a new catering business right here in Sugar Creek called Deep in the Heart Catering. I wanted to introduce myself and my work to some of the people who might need my services in town."

Her harried skepticism turned to enthusiasm as I opened the box with the cherry crumb bars. "I brought a few samples I'd like to share, if that's okay."

She smiled as she peered into the second box I opened, the one with the sandwiches. "You can call me Brenda, hon."

I grabbed a slice of the cherry crumb bar out of the box and handed it to her. She eagerly tasted it, her smile growing bigger as she did. "This is delicious! Hang on a minute, will you?"

A few minutes later, she came back with half a dozen coworkers, all more than willing to try my samples. As they nibbled on sandwiches and bars, I told them about the types of catering I did, emphasizing the flexibility and personalization I offered. When I finished, I left them some cards and sample menus and they thanked me and praised the food.

"Thanks so much for stopping by today, Ms. Hirsch," Brenda said with a smile when everyone else had gone. "We'll definitely be in touch. I have a few things scheduled for the following month that definitely require catering."

As I packed up, leaving behind my contact information, I felt like I'd scored a victory, small yet significant.

After the success I had with Brenda, I made quick work of visiting several other locations in town. Not everyone was as enthusiastic as she had been, but I eventually gave away the last of the sandwiches and sample menus and knew that I'd at least gotten my business some much needed attention. And even though it wasn't all positive, I knew what I'd accomplished today was only the beginning.

Before going back to Primrose House, I made a quick stop at Wild Hare Winery. The sun was just beginning to fade, shooting brilliant orange and purple rays through the sky. It had been a long day, but hope for the future filled me up and made me smile. It was a delightful feeling.

Climbing out of my shiny new van, pride swelled within me. I couldn't resist giving its sleek side a grateful pat before making my way to find Mark and Sheila, and I absently wondered if I shouldn't give it a name.

I found the couple gathering up empty wine bottles and righting chairs on the patio after a busy day of wine tastings. A few customers still lingered near the now repaired patio rail. I waved and smiled.

"Hey, there! I have something exciting to show you both if you've got a few minutes."

They nodded and followed me out to the lot. "Look at what I got myself!" As they checked out the spacious interior, I told them about my car dying and Ryan coming to the rescue.

"Well, I'm sorry we couldn't lend you the van yesterday, but it looks like it was a blessing in disguise!" Mark told me, his eyes twinkling. Sheila nodded, her gaze sweeping over the van with an approving eye.

"I also stopped by because I wanted to chat about your fondue idea for a few minutes," I said as we headed back over to the patio so they could monitor things with the few remaining customers. Sheila and I sat at a table under the wisteria and Mark left to finish cleaning up.

As the sun set over the ridge and lit the vineyards below in gold, Sheila and I made our plans.

"So we'll do three different types of fondue, each paired with a signature wine. I'll do the same buffet style setup and people can come and go."

Sheila nodded. "Let me get the three wines for you so you can taste and figure out what would pair best with each." She hopped up and went into the house, returning a few minutes later with three bottles of wine.

I grinned. Life as a caterer wasn't always enjoyable. There was plenty of struggle and uncertainty. But sometimes it *was*. I'd get Cassie to help me taste things and we could have a night of it. Sheila and I agreed on doing our event two weeks from the following Saturday, which she thought would be enough time to get the proper marketing buzz going.

Mark had come back midway through our discussion and pulled out a chair. He waited until Sheila and I had hashed out the fondue party details and then asked, "Can you tell us what's been going on with the murder investigation? Anything new?"

I sighed, the weight of the recent events pressing down on me. "Ugh, it's a nightmare. You wouldn't believe all that's happened. You heard Tori died, right? That someone killed her at Primrose House?"

They nodded, their faces drawn with interest and concern. "Well," I continued, "Ryan figured out who killed Barry, and it turns out it wasn't one of the original group at all, but the couple who were staying at the B&B at the same time!"

The shock registered clearly on their faces, a mix of disbelief and intrigue. "Ryan thinks they might have been working with someone else in the group, especially now that Tori is dead. But so far, he hasn't found any solid evidence to prove anyone else was involved."

Sheila's expression turned thoughtful, a crease forming between her brows as she thought. "Now that you mention it, I remember the couple was here with another person from that group of yours."

"You mean the day of the party?" I asked, trying to piece together her recollection with the timeline of events.

"No, they were here together the day before. The three of them sat over at the big table near the rail that broke..." Sheila's voice trailed off, her gaze distant as she revisited the memory.

My eyes widened, a jolt of realization shooting through me. "Which one was it? Was it a man or a woman?"

"It was the young woman, not the icy blonde, but the other one."

Cheryl.

"Wow. This seems very important. I'm not sure it means anything, but I'll call Ryan right now and let him know. Thanks, Sheila." I was already reaching for my phone, the urgency of the situation lending speed to my movements as I said a quick goodbye and started for the parking lot.

"Good luck, honey. Let us know what happens," Sheila cried after me, concern in her voice.

I dialed Ryan's number as I pulled out of the Wild Hare parking lot, my mind racing with possibilities. This new information could be the key to unraveling the mystery, and I felt a deep responsibility to pass on the information quickly. The wait for the call to connect was agonizing, each ring echoing my escalating heartbeat.

But of course I got his voicemail greeting instead of his reassuring voice. I left a message detailing what Sheila had revealed, each word heavy with the weight of its implications.

The drive back was a whirlwind of thoughts, my mind racing as I tried to piece together the puzzling connections. Why would Cheryl have been with Jeff and his wife at the winery? The question gnawed at me, an itch I couldn't scratch. Unless there was a prior acquaintance between them, their association made little sense.

Pulling into the parking lot, Cassie's truck was a welcome

sight. A sigh escaped me—I desperately needed my sleuthing part-
ner, now more than ever.

My mind wandered back to the coworking space and the
heated exchange between Cheryl and Tori. Tori's words echoed in
my memory. *"I know about your brother."* There was a clue there, a
piece of the puzzle that was just out of reach, teasing the edges of
my understanding.

It was as I cut the engine that a sudden realization struck me
like a bolt of lightning. Cheryl's bracelet—the initials C.H.M. The
'H'—her maiden name...could it be Hildebrand? The pieces of the
puzzle slammed into place with a clarity that took my breath away.
Could Cheryl be related to Jeff Hildebrand? Was this the missing
link that tied everything together?

As I stepped out of the car, the warm evening air added to my
heated thoughts and I felt like I was burning up. The pieces were
coming together, and with each step towards Primrose House, I
braced myself for the unraveling mystery that awaited.

I breezed into the house, the box of leftover samples cradled in
my arms, and let out a sigh when I found Cassie, Bertie, and Aunt
Meg casually flipping through magazines at the kitchen counter.

"Y'all! I think I just figured it out," I whispered, the words
tumbling out in a hush of excitement and nerves, my eyes scanning
the room as if the walls themselves could betray us.

Cassie's eyes widened, a spark of intrigue lighting them up,
while Bertie gave me a quizzical look, her head tilting slightly. "Figured out what?" she asked, her voice a mix of curiosity and
concern.

Gathering my thoughts, I laid out the pieces of the puzzle that
had finally clicked together in my mind. "I think Cheryl is Jeff
Hildebrand's sister. She got a job at NexTech Dynamics just to
help her brother exact revenge on Barry for stealing his technology.
And once Tori found out about her brother, Tori had to be killed
too." The words felt surreal as they hung in the air. It was a theory

that sounded like something out of a crime thriller, yet every instinct told me it was true.

Before we could process the gravity of what I'd just said, a high voice, tinged with anxiety and malice, cut through the tension from behind us. "Looks like you people solved the mystery after all. Congratulations."

CHAPTER TWENTY-SIX

Cheryl's sudden intrusion sent a jolt through the room, and an icy shiver raced up my spine as she emerged from the shadowy space of the hallway. The four of us froze as we realized she'd overheard our conversation. The pleasant mask she'd worn around us the last week was gone, her face now harsh and hostile. There was a hardened glint in her eye and her mouth twisted into a chilling smile, devoid of any warmth.

"I thought it would be easier here," she began, her voice low and menacing as she advanced towards us. "I thought this little town was the perfect place for Jeff to confront Barry. You all seemed so innocent. So... inept."

The rudeness of her words left me speechless. Despite now knowing the depth of her malice, her audacity still took me aback. Even in the face of danger, a part of me bristled at her dismissal of our community. How dare she talk about Sugar Creek that way? Her contempt not only for us but for the place we called home added an extra layer of offense to an already tense situation.

I was completely over it. There was no way she was getting away with the murder or the insult.

"The man who stayed here last week with his wife was your

brother, wasn't he?" I asked her. Despite knowing the danger she posed, my need for answers overpowered my caution. I didn't want to provoke her into doing something crazy, but boy, I wanted to know a few things for sure. "You planned on killing Barry with him, didn't you?"

"He wasn't supposed to kill Barry. He only wanted to scare him," she cried. Her face moved from anger to pain. "Jeff lost everything when Barry stole his technology. The money... it would've helped our family in ways you can't imagine. Our mom was sick and there were medical bills we couldn't pay. That's why Jeff worked so hard on building the technology in the first place. But when Innocore imploded, Jeff lost it all. And so did our family."

Her words painted a picture of desperation and her story tugged at my heart, but it didn't justify their actions. "That's no excuse for killing someone," I reasoned, my voice firm yet heavy with the weight of the situation.

She stepped further into the kitchen, her hands waving wildly. "Jeff didn't want to kill him! He only wanted to confront him, to make him realize how much he'd hurt us. He wanted Barry to apologize and to give him his due. Give him a piece of the new company. It must've been an accident what happened at the winery. It wasn't part of the plan we discussed."

"That isn't true, though, because the two of you met at the winery the day before the dinner party. And one, or both, of you destroyed that railing. If the railing would've held, Barry never would've died. It was intentional."

She waved a hand at me, clearly fed up with my logic. "It went too far, you're right. But Barry deserved what he got in the end. Either way, I had nothing to do with that part. I just told Jeff the plans for NexTech's travel and made sure he had access to confront him."

"But you killed Tori, though, right?" I asked, the words heavy in the air between us.

Her expression twisted into a sour smile, contorting her features into something almost unrecognizable—harsh and cold. "Tori deserved what she got. She was an awful person, never satisfied, never happy, never friendly. So, when she found out about Jeff, it wasn't hard for me to make my decision. I would do anything for my brother."

As the reality of her confession sunk in, a chill ran through the room. I could almost feel Aunt Meg, Bertie, and Maria stiffen and the tension suddenly spiked. I started to pull my cell phone out of my pocket to call Ryan, but Cheryl was faster, her movements alarmingly quick.

Like a shadow, she flew to the counter and seized my chef's knife. Holding it up, she turned to Aunt Meg, who sat frozen at the bar, the color draining from her face. Cheryl's smile transformed into something sly, a menacing glint in her eye as she wielded the knife with a terrifying calm.

The room was thick with fear. Aunt Meg's eyes were wide, her body rigid as she faced the imminent threat. Bertie and Maria exchanged panicked glances, their minds racing for a way out of the dire situation we found ourselves in. I could see Bertie subtly inching closer to her cellphone that sat on the counter, her movements deliberate yet cautious, trying not to draw Cheryl's attention away from me.

But Cheryl's actions were swift and calculated. She noticed Bertie's movement towards the phone and closed the distance to Aunt Meg with alarming speed. "Put the phone down. You're not calling anybody," she demanded, her voice laced with a chilling authority. She grabbed Aunt Meg's arm, yanking her to stand with a force that made her wince. I could see the fear in Aunt Meg's eyes, the pain etched on her face from Cheryl's tight grip.

My heart pounded as my hand froze on my pocket. Slowly, I raised my hands, showing Cheryl that I wouldn't make any sudden moves. "Okay, okay, just don't hurt her," I pleaded, my voice barely a whisper. The safety of Aunt Meg was my only priority, even as every instinct screamed for me to act.

Cheryl's eyes darted around the room, calculating her next move. "Keys," she hissed, her gaze now locked on mine. "Give me the car keys, now!" Her demand was clear, and the implication of her next steps dawned on me. She planned to take Aunt Meg with her as a hostage to secure her escape.

I hesitated, the weight of the situation pressing down on me. Aunt Meg gave me a look, a mixture of fear and reassurance, as if to say it would be okay, even though we both knew the danger she was about to face. With a heavy heart, I nodded to where the keys hung by the door, unwilling to risk making a move that could provoke Cheryl further.

As Cheryl dragged Aunt Meg toward the side kitchen door, I felt a helplessness wash over me. My mind raced, desperate for a way to resolve the situation without further endangering Aunt Meg. The sight of them stepping out into the uncertain safety of the early evening, with Cheryl's firm grip on Aunt Meg, was a moment I knew would haunt me. I had to find a way to help Aunt Meg, to bring her back safely.

The door clicked shut behind them, leaving a silence that echoed with the gravity of what had just unfolded. My resolve hardened; I couldn't let Cheryl win. I had to act, and fast, to save Aunt Meg and stop Cheryl once and for all.

"Call Ryan!" I shouted, my voice tinged with desperation as I darted out the door to follow them. My eyes caught Cheryl frantically pressing the car key button, her movements erratic as she tried to figure out which vehicle responded to the remote. And, of course, it was my brand new catering van.

Dragging Aunt Meg across the parking lot, Cheryl's grip was unyielding. The sound of Aunt Meg's cries pierced the evening air, each sob a sharp stab to my heart. Fueled by a mix of fear and determination, I sprinted towards them, hoping to intercept

Cheryl before she could whisk Aunt Meg away to who knew where in my van.

Just as Cheryl was about to force Aunt Meg into the back of the van, a sudden blare of sirens sliced through the tension. Ryan's cruiser barreled into the lot, its lights flashing a furious red and blue, followed closely by two other police cars.

"Stop right where you are," Ryan commanded, his voice booming across the parking lot as he emerged from his vehicle, his gun trained on Cheryl with unwavering precision.

The urgency of the moment hung heavy in the air, a tension that seemed to freeze time itself. Cheryl halted, her plan thwarted by the sudden appearance of law enforcement, and Aunt Meg slumped against the van as Cheryl dropped the knife and Aunt Meg's arm. I stood rooted where I was, my breath caught in my throat, as the realization of how close we had come to disaster settled over me.

In the charged silence that followed Ryan's command, Cheryl seemed to crumble, her body language shifting from defiance to resignation as the officers approached, handcuffs ready. The swift efficiency with which they arrested her, securing her hands behind her back, seemed almost too easy after the last tense minutes we'd spent with her.

As they led Cheryl away, her head bowed, a mix of emotions played across her face—regret, defiance, perhaps even relief at the end of her desperate attempt to escape justice.

Ryan paused before following Cheryl to the cruiser, his gaze meeting mine. "I'll be back as soon as I can," he promised. "I'll need y'all's statements, but first I need to have some words with Cheryl." He squeezed my hand in reassurance and I flew to Aunt Meg as his vehicle pulled out of the lot.

Aunt Meg's face was covered in tears and I pulled her to me, needing the comfort of having her in my arms after such a close call. I don't know what I would have done if something had happened to her. Supporting her trembling form as we made our way back to the safety of Primrose House, I let my own tears fall, tears of frustration, terror, and relief, too. The ordeal had taken its toll on us all, but thank goodness it had left Aunt Meg physically unharmed.

"I'm so sorry, Aunt Meg," I whispered, my voice thick with emotion. "I'm so glad you're safe."

She leaned into me as we climbed the front stairs, where Cassie and Bertie waited for us. As we all came together in a group hug, I felt a huge weight lift off our collective shoulders. At long last, we had the promise of resolution, and perhaps even peace on the horizon.

Chapter Twenty-Seven

It took a lot of effort after the night we'd had, but the next morning, Cassie, Maria, Maria's daughter Daniela, and I swung into full gear to put Aunt Meg's birthday party together. Thick clouds hung in the far distance again, but I willfully ignored them. Nothing else was going to get in the way of me throwing this shindig.

"I don't know if I've ever seen so much bunting in my life," Cassie declared as she twisted the pink paper around and around the banister. I glanced up from the homemade sign I was struggling to make just perfect and my eyebrows shot up.

"Goodness. It's certainly festive in here," I said with a laugh. While I wasn't paying attention, Cassie and Daniela had wrapped just about every surface with pink, purple, and orange paper.

"It'll do Aunt Meg good. She needs a little more festive spirit. Especially after the week she's had."

As much as I'd wanted to wait for Aunt Meg's party so she could have a little recovery time after all that had happened, we were on a deadline because one of Bertie's children had decided to visit her in Spoonbill Bay only a few days later and she had to get home. There was no time to dilly-dally if we wanted to include Bertie in the festivities.

I made a final flourish of marker on the hot pink sign and then went to check on the cupcakes in the oven. They were Aunt Meg's favorite—cinnamon spice—and the spices smelled delicious as I opened the oven and poked one with a toothpick.

Maria came in with an armload of sheets as I was pulling the last pan of cupcakes out. She headed to the laundry room and then returned a minute later with a smile on her face. "It smells wonderful. I hope you made enough," she said, her mouth lifting up in the corner.

I laughed and looked around the kitchen, where nearly every available countertop held muffin trays. "I know, it's a lot, right? But I had Ellie's pans from the party still, and I figured I might as well go all out. I have a feeling that between Aunt Meg's friends and nosy locals who want all the juicy details of her brush with death, we're going to have quite the crowd tonight."

Maria leaned on the counter and I handed her a tiny piece of one cupcake as I split it to test. I popped another piece into my own mouth and smiled. Just the right mix of cinnamon, nutmeg, cloves, and vanilla.

"These are incredible, Abby. I must have the recipe."

"How is cleanup going upstairs?" I'd hoped it wouldn't take her long to turn over the guest rooms so she could help to set up tables outside.

"Almost done. The laundry is the last thing, but I can help right now until the sheets finish washing."

Kevin and Eric, the two remaining employees of NexTech Dynamic, had packed up and left less than an hour after Ryan gave them the all clear the evening before and we were all thrilled to have Primrose House to ourselves once again. Aunt Meg hadn't even seen them off, but had stayed in her room until they were gone, which was a first for her. I couldn't blame her one bit, though. It was hard enough for *me* to make eye contact as I'd checked them out. The whole ordeal had shaken us all up.

An hour later, Maria and I put the last chair under the tables outside just as Bertie's car pulled up. She and Aunt Meg got out and came around the side of the house. Aunt Meg's eyes held tears as she took in the party spread.

"Abby, you didn't have to go to all this trouble."

I pulled her in for a hug. "Of course I did. You deserve a party more than anyone I know. You're always so kind, so generous with your time and your space. We are all grateful that you're in our lives."

She wiped tears away as she pulled back and gave everyone who had gathered a smile. "Thank you all for coming and for making my birthday a special one. Goodness knows I need a little uplift in my life right now." Right as she said it, the band near the oak tree started up. She threw her head back and laughed.

It didn't take long for Aunt Meg to get lost in the crowd. She was the star of the evening and everyone had to say hello and to hear the story of her hostage crisis. After keeping her company for a bit longer I headed inside to take stock of the food situation.

Kids ran through the house and yard and Cocoa ran after them, his tongue lolling and his little legs carrying him as fast as they could go. He was living his best life, and I knew he'd be good and tuckered by the time Cassie and I took him home.

Piles of potluck dishes sat on every available sideboard, my now iced cupcakes the center of attention. I noticed several holes in my artful display. No doubt the kids who now ran willy-nilly had fueled up on them before their play.

Ryan and Ty came in from the front as I added more cupcakes to the stand. Ty nodded to me and smiled. "Is Cassie around?"

"She's out back," I told him. Ryan set a small wrapped present on the table along with several others and then came around the kitchen island for a lengthy kiss. At long last, he wasn't in his sheriff's uniform and he was once again a private citizen. And free to act like my boyfriend in public. I wrapped my arms around his neck and leaned my cheek against his chest. "Thanks for coming."

"Are you kidding? I wouldn't miss it. How's the van treating you?"

He snagged a piece of cheese from a platter and gazed hungrily around at all the food.

"It's a dream, Ryan. I can't thank you enough, really. And I can't thank you enough for saving Aunt Meg last night."

He waved my comment away. "No need to thank me. Really. I'm just glad y'all are safe."

We each grabbed a plate of food and went out to the yard to join Aunt Meg and the others.

I could tell Aunt Meg was trying to be cheerful and enjoy the party, but in reality, her mind was miles away and her nerves shot. How could they not be? She'd been held hostage less than twenty-four hours before. All morning while I was arranging things, I'd thought the party would help bring her spark back, help take her mind off things. Now I could see that more than anything, it'd just worn her out even more. Guilt pressed down on me as I struggled to think of a way to cheer her.

"I've been doing a lot of thinking after everything that's happened. And I think I need a break," she said as Ryan and I joined the group.

"What? What do you mean?" I asked.

Every eye was on her suddenly and she stared down at her hands, overwhelmed by the attention.

She sighed. "I need a break from the B&B business. The last couple of weeks were too much for me. I can't bring myself to do it again come Saturday when the next load of guests arrive. Bertie and I talked a while this afternoon and we've decided it would be good for me to go back to Spoonbill Bay with her for a spell. Take some time off. I can fly home when I'm ready or she can bring me back. I'll cancel my upcoming reservations for the next few weeks at least, see how it goes."

I tried hard to keep the shock from my face. Aunt Meg, leaving Sugar Creek? It was almost unimaginable.

But that was a problem, I realized. Aunt Meg deserved rest and relaxation as much or more than any guest that came through her door. She shouldn't spend every waking hour tending to other people's needs.

"I know that's a really hard decision for you, Aunt Meg. But I know, too, that you absolutely deserve a break." I sighed and looked out on all the happy people dancing and talking and eating under the trees and contemplated what I was about to say. But there was no real decision to make. I knew it was the right thing to do. "You don't have to cancel your reservations. I'll move in and take care of things while you're away."

Her eyes darted to me. "I can't ask so much, girly. You have your own business to run. I don't want my burnout to get in the way of your success."

I smiled. "It won't. Who knows, maybe being here all the time will actually help me get more done? Besides, it's not like I'm swimming in business right now."

Maria chimed in. "I can help as well. I know Primrose House very well now. And Daniela is getting older," she said as she scanned the crowd of kids and found her daughter with a smile. "I can start working more hours. It will be fine, Meg. Abby and I can handle things while you're away."

Aunt Meg put her hands up to her face. Her shoulders shook. We were all silent, letting her have her moment. "Y'all are too much, you know that?" she said as she stood and came around to my side of the table and pulled me into a hug.

"No, we aren't. We're just doing what you would do for any of us. Now you go and pack your bags. Stay as long as you like. We'll handle it all while you're away."

A wide grin broke out on her face. "Talk about a birthday present! Alright, if y'all are sure."

"We're sure," I told her and squeezed her hand.

She headed toward the house to pack her things, and I turned toward Cassie. "Hey, now you get your place back to yourself! No more Abby ruining date night!"

Ryan and Ty both laughed, but Cassie frowned. "I told you already I like you staying with me. You better promise to come back as soon as your aunt gets home."

Laughing, I leaned into Ryan, who wrapped his arm around me. "I promise. I guess we'll have to share custody of Cocoa for the time being."

She glanced over to our dog, who lounged in the dirt under a tree, his tongue hanging all the way out. He looked like he'd finally hit a wall, but he was one happy critter. "I bet he'll like that. Always something new. Plenty of attention."

Ryan turned to Bertie. "What about you, Bertie? Do you have any more adventures coming up now that you're headed home?"

"You never know. This visit sure has been interesting," Bertie replied with a sly smile. Something in the way she winked at me made me think she might just have caught a sleuthing bug on her visit to Sugar Creek. I hope it didn't make her too sick.

Ryan squeezed my shoulder and then stood and stretched. "That was delicious, y'all. Thanks so much for having me. But I think it's time to get back to the station. We've finished the investigation, but now comes the fun part...the paperwork." He rolled his eyes, and I laughed. Ty groaned, then gave Cassie a quick peck and stood as well.

Maria, Cassie, Bertie, and I sat there watching the party go on around us and made small talk, although I could tell we all had an awful lot of mixed emotions going on. It was a lot to process—the troublesome guests, the murders, the upheaval, and now Aunt Meg's departure. It would take some time for us all to recover.

Aunt Meg came back as the party was winding down. She looked more peaceful than I'd seen her in a long time. I was worried about how things would go with her gone, but I was happy she would get the chance to take a break.

"Well, I hate to leave y'all," Bertie said with a sad smile. "But I need a vacation from my vacation! This week has been one big ball of stress, if I'm honest," she finished with a laugh. "It's back to beach life for me!"

Cassie, Bertie, Maria, and I all stood and huddled around Aunt Meg, pulling her in for a group hug. We stood there together for a minute, all us sleuthing ladies in a tight bond that wouldn't ever break. I knew I was lucky to have them all. Aunt Meg might leave for a while, but she'd be with us in spirit.

My only question now was, could I really handle both her business and mine?

Only time would tell.

———

I hoped you enjoyed your time in Sugar Creek! Want to know what happens with Abby when Aunt Meg leaves Primrose House for vacation? Check out book 4, Death and Blackberry Pie.

Order Death and Blackberry Pie now!

A cozy B&B in need of a caretaker's touch. A catering job with a deadly surprise. A small town stirred by secrets and suspense.

After her Aunt Meg decides to take a much needed break from the B&B business, Abby Hirsch steps up to fill her shoes at the quaint Primrose House B&B while juggling her new catering business as well. But her plans for both businesses are quickly upended when a routine catering job turns into a deadly investigation, with a shocking discovery at a client's home leaving the town reeling.

With the town abuzz over whispers of love and imminent surprises, Abby finds herself kneading through secrets and lies, where even the sweetest blackberry pie can hide bitter truths. As she joins forces with her best friend Cassie and the charming Sheriff Ryan Iverson, the sleuthing team embarks on a quest to peel back layers of deceit, ensuring that in this small town, justice will be served alongside Abby's delectable dishes.

Order Death and Blackberry Pie now!

Read on for an excerpt of Death and Blackberry Pie!

———

Want more cozy fun in your inbox?

I send out a newsletter twice a month with personal stories, giveaways, recipes, polls, reading recommendations, and other fun surprises – along with the latest updates on my books!

I'd love to stay connected with you. Follow the link below to subscribe.

Subscribe To Nova's Newsletter
https://novawalsh.com/novas-newsletter/

Swiss Fondue

INGREDIENTS

1 clove garlic, minced
8 oz dry white wine (Pinot Grigio and Sauvignon Blanc work well)
1 tsp lemon juice
8 oz Gruyere cheese, grated
8 oz Emmentaler cheese, grated
1 tsp corn flour
1/2 tsp ground nutmeg
1/2 tsp black pepper

DIRECTIONS

In a fondue pot or saucepan, stir together garlic, wine, and lemon juice. Heat until bubbling then reduce heat to low. Mix the grated cheeses together and dust with corn flour and spices, tossing to coat the cheese as much as possible.

Add cheese a little at a time to the pot, stirring to melt with each addition. I know it looks delicious and you want to hurry and eat it, but the longer you take to do this step the better. You never want the cheese to boil, only melt.

Once all the cheese has melted, give each guest a fondue fork or regular fork along with items to dip (see notes for suggestions) and let them go to it. Just remember to watch the cheese and turn it down if it begins to boil.

NOTES/VARIATIONS

A great variation on this classic fondue is to use cheddar and beer. Simply replace the wine with beer (darker more flavorful beer such as Ambers or IPA work well), the Gruyere and Emmentaler with sharp or extra-sharp cheddar, and omit the nutmeg.

The classic fondue dipper is cubes of French bread, although many creative variations can be used. Try roasted baby potatoes or other Roasted Vegetables, fresh broccoli, cherry tomatoes, or chunks of chicken breast.

Monster Cookies

INGREDIENTS

1 stick butter (1/4 cup), softened

1 cup brown sugar

1 cup white sugar

3 eggs

1 1/2 cups peanut butter

2 tsp baking soda

5 cups quick cook oatmeal

1 cup chocolate chips

1/2 cup dried cranberries or dried cherries

DIRECTIONS

Preheat the oven to 350 degrees

Cream together the butter and sugars

Add in eggs one at a time and then the peanut butter and mix well

Add baking soda and mix and then the oatmeal and mix(find a sturdy spoon--you'll need some muscles for this part!)

Add in the chocolate chips and fruit and mix

Drop in large tablespoons onto a greased pan and bake around 10 minutes, until cooked through

These cookies are gluten free and versatile! Try add ins like nuts, fruit, and white or dark chocolate chips to change it up.

German Potato Salad

INGREDIENTS

2 lb potatoes (russets or red potatoes work well)

1 Tbsp lemon juice

1 Tbsp red wine or cider vinegar

1/4 cup olive oil

2 tsp dijon or whole grain mustard

1 garlic clove

2 tsp salt (this is a rough estimate--salt to taste)

1/2 red onion, thinly sliced

2 Tbsp capers

diced fresh herbs (parsley, dill, chives and basil all work well, if no fresh herbs available use dried)

DIRECTIONS

Clean and peel potatoes (leave peel on if using thin skinned potatoes) and boil in a large pot of salted water until tender

Whisk lemon juice, vinegar, mustard, salt, and garlic together and then slowly drizzle in the olive oil while whisking

Add herbs to the oil and vinegar if using

Once the potatoes are cooked, chop them into bite sized pieces and drizzle with the dressing
Add in sliced red onions and capers and top with more herbs

This salad is best if made a little ahead of time to let the dressing really soak in but, it's still good right after it's made!

DEATH AND BLACKBERRY PIE -
CHAPTER ONE

I'm from Texas, and one of the reasons I like Texas is because there's no one in control.

It wouldn't be long before I found out how true that Willy Nelson quote was. But as my best friend Cassie and I navigated the steep rocky path down toward our destination on a sweltering Wednesday in the middle of August, trouble was very far from my mind.

We followed carefully behind my boyfriend, Ryan Iverson, and Cassie's boyfriend Ty Clayburn, as we made our way to a little-known swimming hole about half an hour from Sugar Creek. The guys flew down the difficult path like it was another day in the park but Cassie and I picked our way down the limestone and scrub-brush at a snail's pace, watching for snakes and cactus, and gabbing nonstop.

"Aunt Meg called last night," I said, adjusting my grip on the vintage picnic basket I carried. The pretty wood weave had caught my eye at an estate sale, but as I shuffled the heavy bulk of it back and forth between my hands, I regretted not packing our lunch in something more practical. "She's having a great time in Spoonbill Bay with Bertie. They went jet skiing yesterday. Can you believe it?" I told her with a laugh.

My Aunt Meg, the spirited owner of Primrose House B&B, decided to take an extended vacation to visit her cousin Roberta on the gulf coast after a traumatic incident where she was held hostage by a deranged woman. The experience had shaken her more than she'd let on, and after a lot of persuading she finally agreed to take a break in Spoonbill Bay with Bertie.

Before leaving, she'd entrusted me with the responsibility of running the B&B, a decision that made both of us a bit uneasy. Aunt Meg's absence meant that I was juggling the B&B's daily operations along with my own small fledgling catering business. Thankfully, I wasn't alone in this endeavor. Aunt Meg's trusted helper, Maria, was a lifesaver. In fact, Maria was so capable that she practically managed the B&B by herself.

Cassie chuckled, brushing a strand of hair from her sweaty forehead. "That Bertie could talk a rattlesnake out of its own skin. Did they have fun? Or was Meg scared to death? I bet she was scared to death."

"A little bit of both, I'd say. It's been really good for her. She keeps asking if she should come home but I can tell she isn't quite ready so I keep telling her no."

"And y'all are holding it together so far right?" Cassie asked, eyeing the path ahead. "I'm sure it's hard for her to let loose on the reins after all these years. She's been the sole caretaker for Primrose House for a long time now."

I nodded. "Mostly holding it together," I said, huffing a bit as the weight of the picnic basket made my arms ache. "I don't know what I'd do without Maria. But I've got a couple of big catering jobs coming up and more guests this coming weekend. It's a lot to handle. But I'm sure we'll pull through like we always do."

Cassie gave me a sympathetic look. "You've got this, Abby. If anyone can juggle multiple businesses, it's you."

I smiled, appreciating her confidence. "Thanks, Cass. I just hope I can keep juggling and not drop a ball." We were nearly at the end of the trek down and the guys were so far ahead of us that I could barely make them out. I took the opportunity of the distance to pry a little. "How was the trip to Dallas?"

Cassie blushed slightly, glancing at Ty who was just coming to the end of the trail. "It was fun for the most part. But meeting his sisters was intimidating! It felt very serious. But they were all so nice. They'd fit right into our crowd."

I laughed softly. "Well, it sounds like things are moving in a good direction with you two."

We arrived at the end of the path and started the final climb down. It was rocky and took plenty of concentration not to slip. But once we finally passed through the last of the scrubby cedar trees and sharp rocks, the river opened up in front of us and I stopped and smiled, appreciating the scene. The river was wide and shallow, with an outcropping of rocks toward the east where small groups of sunbathers sprawled out and splashed.

Ryan set down the intertubes he'd been carrying at a shady spot under a big oak tree and turned back to me with a smile, holding out his hand to help me down the final difficult rock. With a grateful sigh I finally set the picnic basket down and stretched, then pulled my coverup over my head. It was so hot I was already sweating through it and I couldn't wait to get into the cool river water.

Catching Ryan peeking at me in my bathing suit with undisguised interest, I blushed and looked away, suddenly not wanting to make eye contact. I appreciated his gaze, and I was happy that he was interested, but it still made me a little uncomfortable. Everything with him was still so new. It would take some getting used to, being in a real relationship with him.

We made our way over to the sandy strip next to the water and I sighed and closed my eyes as I stuck my feet in. Heavenly.

"Woo!" Cassie called as she hopped down onto the sand with us. "That was a workout!"

She laughed as Ty grabbed her and swung her around. "So worth it though!" he replied as he pulled her toward the water. "That river's gonna feel so good, honey!"

Laughing as they both ran toward the river bank like kids, I shaded my eyes and scanned the river. It was a weekday so thankfully it wasn't overly crowded. Ryan came up behind me and wrapped his arms around me, his bare chest connecting with my bare shoulders. I sure could get used to this.

"You want to float, or should we eat something first?"

I grinned and turned to give him a sideways kiss. "Let's float. The water feels so good."

He grabbed two intertubes and we awkwardly settled our bodies into them. The cool river water was a shock, but only for a second. I quickly grew accustomed as I splashed and floated my way toward where Cassie and Ty were wading.

We floated gently down the river, the cool water a refreshing contrast to the scorching August sun. Laughter and splashing filled the air as we drifted along, occasionally bumping into each other and playfully shoving off again. Cassie and Ty were in their own world, splashing each other and giggling like children, while Ryan and I floated side by side, our hands occasionally brushing as we maneuvered our tubes.

"Isn't this perfect?" Cassie called out, her face glowing with happiness. "I can't remember the last time I felt this relaxed."

"Me either," I admitted, letting the current carry me. "It's nice to just float and not think about anything for a while."

Ryan leaned back in his tube, closing his eyes and letting out a contented sigh. "This is the life. Good company, beautiful scenery, and no worries." It made me happy to see him so relaxed. With the safety of Sugar Creek always on his shoulders, he rarely had the chance to unwind. Ryan's dedication to his work as the town's sheriff often left him tense and preoccupied, but here, floating in the river with the three of us, he seemed to shed all those burdens. It was a side of him I cherished.

We floated in companionable silence for a while longer. The sun sparkled on the surface of the river. Every so often, a fish would dart by, a flash of silver in the clear water. Children jumped from a rock nearby, sending up sprays of water and shrieks as they hit the coolness. It was the height of relaxation and I soaked it up.

After a long while of floating in the river, I finally decided it was time to eat. Heading toward the shore in my tube I called out, "I made something special for y'all if you're ready to eat!"

The group quickly followed me out of the water toward our spot and watched as I dug through the picnic basket to the very bottom and pulled out a large pie carrier. "This is for after lunch," I told them with a sly smile. "It's a blackberry pie. I made it just this morning."

Ryan groaned and Ty licked his lips. Seemed I would have some takers. I'd gotten up early just for the pie, making the dough by hand and mixing the plump berries with sugar, cinnamon, nutmeg, and butter before sealing it with pretty crimping on the edges and baking it. Then I'd let it cool for as long as I could before I'd packed the rest of our picnic for the day's adventure. It had been a chore to make and an even bigger chore to lug down to the river, but the efforts were well worth it.

Cassie helped me spread out a picnic blanket and we put out the cheese, meat, and cracker spread she'd made for the day. It looked delicious, with hard cheese, salami, dried fruit, and nuts. I added in an olive tapenade and baguette I'd picked up from the Sugar Creek Bakery and we tucked into our feast.

Midway through lunch, I realized that Ryan was giving Ty strange looks. I stopped chewing as my eyes bounced from one man to the other. "What's going on with you two?" I finally asked.

They both eyed one another but didn't answer me. "You got

this, man. There's no slack in your rope. You'll be fine," Ryan told Ty with a solemn nod.

I glanced at Cassie and saw that she was nearly bouncing out of her seat with excitement. Something was up, and I wasn't part of it.

Ty cleared his throat and got up on his knees in front of Cassie. He reached into a pocket of his swim trunks and pulled something out and my hands flew to my mouth. Finally, I knew what was going on. Ty was about to propose!

"Cassie, honey," Ty began. I watched as tears sprang to Cassie's eyes. "You know I'm over the moon for ya, don't ya?"

She nodded, and the tears began to fall. He took her hand and squeezed. "Well, I just know without a doubt that you and I were meant to be together. Like Desi and Lucy, right?" he said with a laugh. It warmed me all over. Cassie had always been a huge I Love Lucy fan. Ty did a good one making that reference.

I giggled too, from nervous excitement and the joy I felt surrounding our little group. I leaned back into Ryan and he wrapped his arms around me, kissing the top of my head.

"I know, Ty. I feel the same," Cassie replied.

"Whew!" he cried with a laugh as he opened the box, revealing a beautiful antique engagement ring. "Cause if you didn't, I don't know what I would've done!"

"Ty, buddy. Get on with it," Ryan said, laughter in his voice.

He cleared his throat one last time. "Cassie Divine, you would make me the happiest man alive if you'd agree to be my bride. What do ya think?"

The tears were falling in buckets both from Cassie's eyes and my own. She nodded wildly. "Of course I'll marry you, you silly man! I wouldn't have it any other way!" They kissed and he slipped the ring on her finger. Ryan and I turned away, giving them a little privacy and I busied myself pulling a few more things out of the basket.

"I think this calls for a toast!" I said, reaching for a bottle of white wine I'd snagged from Shiela Connoly at Wild Hare Winery the day before. Cassie beamed and grabbed the plastic cups out of the bag nearby.

"What a great idea!" she said, wiping her eyes. "How'd you know?"

I shrugged. "I had no clue! Just seemed like a good idea!"

I poured us all a glass and we clinked our red solo cups together.

"To Ty and Cassie," Ryan said. "May you both have a wonderful life together."

"And to Abby, for making us such a delicious celebration pie!" Cassie added.

Our blanket was bubbling over with a happy energy. As I sliced up the pie and started serving it on paper plates, Cassie leaned over and squeezed my arm.

"Can you believe it? I had no idea!" She glanced down at the gorgeous oval shaped ring on her finger and giggled.

"Really? It seemed like you were in on the whole thing. I was fixing to be mad at you for leaving me out of it!"

Her eyes shot up. "I swear, I had no idea! But as soon as I saw Ty fidgeting, I started to guess," she told me with a laugh. She helped pass out the pie and we all tucked in. It was delicious, tart and sweet with a little crunch from the sugar-dusted crust.

I couldn't believe it. I knew it would probably come eventually. Cassie and Ty had gotten closer and closer over the months that I'd been back in Sugar Creek. But I sure wasn't expecting it today. We would have to spend some time alone later going over every detail. But for now, we would enjoy this celebration with our men.

We spent another hour or so enjoying the river and each other's company. The men took turns racing each other down the shallow rapids, while Cassie and I sat with our feet in the cool water, already starting to dream up wedding plans.

As the afternoon wore on, I glanced at my watch and sighed. "I hate to be the party pooper, but I should probably head back soon. I've got prep work to do for tomorrow's catering job."

Ryan nodded, pulling himself out of the water. "Yeah, I've got the evening shift starting in a couple of hours too."

We packed up our picnic, still riding high on the excitement of the day. The climb back up was just as treacherous as the descent, but our spirits were so high we hardly noticed the effort. We were all caught up in the magic of the afternoon—the proposal, the celebration, the simple joy of being together.

By the time we reached Ryan's truck, the sun was still high in the sky, but the day was winding down for us. It had been one of those perfect afternoons you wish would last forever.

Order Death and Blackberry Pie Now!

ALSO BY NOVA WALSH

THE SUGAR CREEK MYSTERY SERIES

Love cozy mysteries with a side of delicious treats? Check out my Sugar Creek Mystery Series, where small-town sleuths solve crimes and whip up culinary delights!

Death and Wedding Cake

Death and Peaches

Death and Fondue

Death and Blackberry Pie

Death and Eggnog

Death and Groom's Cake (Coming February 2025)

Christmas in Sugar Creek (Short Story Collection)

THE MOONSTONE BAKERY MYSTERY SERIES

Lava Cake and Lies

Cupcakes and Crime (Coming March 2025)

THE MAPLE GROVE ROMANCE SERIES

The Cozy Corner Book Store

The Sugar Stop Chocolate Shop

About Nova Walsh

Author Nova Walsh writes culinary cozy mysteries full of humor, shenanigans, and friendships that last a lifetime. She mixes in a healthy dose of amateur sleuthing, some slow-burn romance, and a pinch of comedy in every book she writes.

Nova is a former chef/caterer who still loves to cook but loves to write even more. She's an enthusiastic, if not totally successful gardener and loves travel, wine, and hanging out with friends.

Nova lives in central Texas with her husband, son, and two delightfully crazy pups. When she isn't writing, she's often cooking, gardening, hiking, or reading a good book with a pup by her side.

You can contact Nova at nova@novawalsh.com

www.ingramcontent.com/pod-product-compliance
Lightning Source LLC
Chambersburg PA
CBHW061438150726
47987CB00001B/257